D0612513

Adios,
Happy Homeland!

Also by Ana Menéndez

In Cuba I Was a German Shepherd
Loving Che
The Last War

ANA
MENÉNDEZ

*Adios,
Happy Homeland!*

Black Cat
a paperback original imprint of Grove/Atlantic, Inc.
New York

"A Found Poem" is quoted from Alejo Carpentier's *Los Pasos Perdidos* (Madrid, Alianza Editorial, 2008), used with permission from Alianza Editorial and La Fundación Alejo Carpentier, Havana, Cuba.

The José Martí quotations in italics in "The Poet in His Labyrinth" are taken from *José Martí: Selected Writings* (Penguin Classics, 2002) and reprinted with kind permission of the translator, Esther Allen and the publisher.

A version of "You Are the Heirs of All My Terrors" originally appeared in *World Literature Today* (September/October 2010).

A version of "Traveling Fools" first appeared as "Travelling Madness" in *Literature: Craft and Voice*, Volume 1, Fiction, *A New Introduction to Literature* (McGraw-Hill, 2009), edited by Nicholas Delbanco and Alan Cheuse; and as "Traveling Fools" in *Bomb Magazine* (Spring 2009).

A version of "The Melancholy Hour" was originally written for the PEN/Faulkner Gala: "Revelation," Washington, D.C., September 2009.

"The Shunting Trains Trace Iron Labyrinths" appeared in *Boston Review* (May/June 2011)

"The Poet in His Labyrinth" appeared in *Our Stories,* www.ourstories.us (Spring 2011).

"Cojimar" appeared on Anderbo.com (May 2011)

Published simultaneously in Canada
Printed in the United States of America

FIRST EDITION

ISBN: 978-0-8021-7084-2

Black Cat
a paperback original imprint of Grove/Atlantic, Inc.
841 Broadway
New York, NY 10003

Distributed by Publishers Group West

www.groveatlantic.com

11 12 13 14   10 9 8 7 6 5 4 3 2 1

For my two Peters

The first bridge, Constitution Station. At my feet
the shunting trains trace iron labyrinths.
—Jorge Luis Borges

Who is the ignoramus who claims that poetry
is not indispensable to a people?
—José Martí

Contents

CONTENTS

CONTENTS

Adios,
Happy Homeland!

Prologue

The modern reader may well wonder what impels me, an Irishman molded in the nineteenth century, to imagine I have anything to add to the literature of that Caribbean island.[1] It is a fair question and I will try to answer it. I was born in Roscommon, a happy green paradise in the heart of Connaught in the west of Ireland. It is, today, still a gentle land of few people and many lakes and rivers. In fact, the name Roscommon derives from the Irish "Ros," which means land of trees; and "Conman," which does not mean what you think it means. Actually, Conman was the name of our famous Irish saint, who was also the see's first bishop and a man of almost supernatural humility and goodness.[2]

In those days, the woods rolled away to all four corners of the earth. Or so it seemed to me as a boy, whose imagination was not yet sullied by the world of encyclopedias and unyielding fact. It was in those early years that I, encouraged by my sweet mother, came to discover that in the warm waters off the coast of Florida, there existed an island of mysterious beauty and

---

1. Ed. note: Cuba is actually an archipelago (from the Greek αρχιπέλαγος), not an island. See Aleksandr I. Solzhenitsyn, *The Gulag Archipelago*, Volume 1, *An Experiment in Literary Investigation*.
2. Dunstable Ramsay, *Celtic Saints of Britain and Europe* (Ireland: Foilseacháin Creidimh na Céad an Déanaí, 1902).

boundless promise. I became enchanted with Cuba—an unusual enough interest for a boy of that era, but even more odd in my isolated village, where a man who had been to Dublin might be called well-traveled and too much interest in the outside world was considered something of a deviance. My father took pains to dissuade me from this alarming new interest, arguing, with reason, that the history of our own island was a more proper endeavor for a son of Eire. To this end, my father and I spent long hours exploring the banks of the river Shannon and gathering chestnuts amid the red cedar and Monterey pine of Lough Key. In the winter, when the work on the farm eased, we spent the short afternoons exploring Rathcroghan,[3] the old burial site that was also home to the high kings of Ireland. Roscommon was covered in castle ruins, ancient battlements, oddly worked stone. History, it seemed to me, was always threatening to overtake the living. I began to suffer from historical claustrophobia—the weight of that enormous past—but, not wanting to further upset my father, I accompanied him as cheerfully as I could, pretending that we were exploring not the ruins of Ailill and Medb but the ramparts of El Morro, the warm Caribbean lapping below. We lived on a farm at the edge of the great plains of Boyle. The farm had belonged to my grandfather before us and to his father before that and his father in a succession that stretched all the way back to the era of

---

3. "*But I who have written this story, or rather this fable, give no credence to the various incidents related in it. For some things in it are the deceptions of demons, other poetic figments; some are probable, others improbable; while still others are intended for the delectation of foolish men*" (*Táin Bó Cúailnge*).

the kings. My father never claimed to be descended from royalty himself, but he could recite the Quain lineage by memory to the fourteenth century. Quain, you may know, was once spelled in Gaelic O Cuinn, which means "descendant of Conn"—unless you consider the alternative spelling Ó Cuáin, in which case it means "descendant of *Cuán*." In fact, though my father seemed to have a firm grasp of who fathered whom, the name Quain itself suffered several bastardizations through the long winter of illiteracy and English atrocity: O'Quinn, MacQuin, MacCuin, Quine, etc.[4] So who's to say when Quién appeared? And then there are the other variations I discovered in my travels: Cual, Que, O'Como. My own family seems to have settled on the present spelling sometime in the late sixteenth century, when Connaught was broken up by Sir Henry Sidney, the bastard.

Our farm was neither the smallest nor the largest in the village. At one time, when the families had been bigger, most of the land was given over to grazing. By the time I was a boy, some of the outlying parcels had been sold off, and on what remained—about twenty hectares—we grew mostly oats and potatoes. The house itself had grown with each generation until the various additions with their twists and odd steps had come to resemble a maze.

There was only one entrance and one exit and to walk from one to the other took more than forty-five minutes. The outer layers of the house were, naturally, the more modern ones,

---

4. Charles X. Kinbote, *The Book of Surnames* (New York: HarperPerennial, originally published 1854).

and the home aged as you walked inward. When I was a boy, a large porch ringed the house on three sides—I have seen such porches in Varadero—and these were covered in sheets of glass to keep out the cold and magnify the sunlight. There was no other house like it in Roscommon, but I never thought to question why it had been built or where the glass—little known in that era—had come from. There was a door that slid open on casters onto the porch, which was furnished in white wicker; and from there, another door that opened into the next layer of the home. Here you entered a small reception area with a closet to hang wet things. To the right was a dining room—the latest of many—and to the left the kitchen, a modern, bright place with taps for hot and cold water. Through the kitchen and around to the side of the house was a small sitting area, and here the house began its first turn inward, toward its origin. The next passageway also contained a kitchen, or what used to be one. In its time it, too, had been modern. The sink was still there, and so was the pump; and where the black iron stove had been, we had installed a toilet for guests. From there, one passed into a long hallway opening onto the bedrooms. And so the house wound deeper and deeper, around rooms and sitting areas, some of them closed off since before I was born. Above the doors and along the corridors, vitrales and wooden window screens let in the light and air. At the heart of this house, at its very center, representing the original one-room stone house built by Deoradhán O Cuinn sometime after the construction of the great M'Donough castle, there sat an enormous library, with books piled floor to ceiling and more, as I discovered one day, neatly organized and alphabetized under a trapdoor in the floor. A single window on the roof lit the room from above, catching bits of dust in its great shaft of light. Over the door, someone (Deoradhán?) had written, in gold letters: *Cha'n eil mi na m' sgoileir, 's cha'n àill leam a bhi, ma'n d'thuairt a mhadadh-ruadh ris a mhadadh-allaidh.* Which, most would agree, was an odd thing to assert.

In this room, I spent the greater part of my childhood, passing my hands over the cracked leather covers until they stopped at a fresh volume with its promise of new worlds and adventures. I was an only child, born to my parents when they were both over forty years old. Perhaps because they had waited so long, both my parents were unusually protective of me, and their care encouraged in me the quieter pursuits of reading and imaginary worlds. In the early evenings, after my chores and my lessons, I would wind my way through the house back to the library, where I remained until I heard through the walls the faint voice of my mother calling that supper was ready.

It was on one such day, in early winter, that I came across a curious book. The book was unlike any other in that library and I remember being surprised that I had not come upon it earlier. Its cover was made not of leather but of a shiny material that was smooth as glass, but lighter than paper. I brought it down from the shelf, opened it at random, and began reading about a poor farmer who lived in a land far, far away and had three sons named Pedro, Pablo, and Juancito. Pedro was big and fat with a red face and a dullard's gaze. Pablo was sickly and pallid, consumed with envy and jealousy. Juancito was as pretty as a girl and so small that he could hide in his father's boot. Everyone called him Meñique.

If you are not an only child, you cannot imagine the delight that a story of brothers engenders in a solitary boy. I was enthralled and sat very still, reading. I read for hours and when I was finished, I wiped away the tears before my mother—who had been yelling about supper with increasing energy—could see them.

The following day I pulled down the book and again opened it at random. This time I came across a poem of such delicate beauty that again my eyes stung with tears on reading the last lines:

> Farewell! . . . The anchor from the sea ascends,
> The sails are full. . . . The ship breaks clear,
> And with soft quiet motion, wave and water fends.[5]

All that week I returned to the book. It was there that I first saw Morro Castle, sketched against a red sky. The great misty sweep of the Malecón in winter. In that book I learned of a place where there is good sun, and water of foam and sand so fine. I learned that it snows because the door to heaven is open. I saw a hallucinatory world, a pilot who never returned, a pair of audacious roses, and understood that my own yearning for the future, for escape from the long history of Ireland, was a

---

5. Hugh A. Harter, *Gertrudis Gómez de Avellaneda* (Boston: Twayne, 1981).

reaching out for the words now before me. It seemed to me that whoever had written this book had written it especially for me.[6]

The book I am talking about, of course, is *A Brief History of the Cuban Poets,* written by Victoria O'Campo at the start of the republic in 1902—the wound, as they say, preceding the blow. I did not dare remove this book from Deoradhán's library. Perhaps I was afraid it would turn to dust—I had read a story about a man who finds a splendid ancient costume hanging in his attic only to have it crumble at his touch. So I was careful not to love the book too much. But I did not stop reading it. For many years, through the Irish winters and the disappointing harvests, I returned again and again to the library to open its covers once more. It is curious now to think about it, but I don't believe I ever reached the end of the book. Perhaps I was afraid of the hollow that exists at the conclusion of every story, the disconsolate sense of loss.

I expected to live out my years in Roscommon, with Cuba remaining a boyhood dream. But as I grew, I learned that the desire to escape—the longing for wings—was not a private fantasy. While I read my strange book, Ireland was becoming a country of emigrants, too, and at the close of my seventeenth year, I had my chance. An uncle on my father's side was shipping out to Mexico the following summer and invited me to come

---

6. *"To transcend experience and to reach a world of Things-in-Themselves, I agree, is impossible. But does it follow that the whole universe in every sense is a possible object of my experience?"* F. H. Bradley, *Appearance and Reality* (London: S. Sonnenschein; New York: Macmillan, 1893, pp. 215–217).

along. I would pay my board and transport by working in the ship's kitchen. I hesitated, being a good son, and not wanting to leave my old parents on the farmstead by themselves. But they insisted—both understood that my prospects for a career and marriage were slim in Roscommon—and on a clear day in June, one of the warmest on record, we set sail for the New World.

The March Warbler was not a large ship, and the journey took an entire month. The passengers were an odd lot. Some of them were very tall and so white as to be almost translucent; others were dark and slender, their women veiled. I met up regularly with such a couple on deck, after the evening meal. In halting French, they told me they were fleeing the Ottomans. The woman, who did not speak as often as the man, had relatives in Mexico, and that is where they were headed. At first, I doubted their fantastic story—being chased from their home, gathering their things in the dark, fleeing with only a few kurus sewn into their shoes and hems. But as the journey progressed, I learned that such stories were common on that ship.

We arrived in Havana on the first of August; it was the most beautiful land that human eyes had ever seen. I bade my uncle farewell—he was traveling on to Mexico—and set about making for myself a new life. I worked for a while as a shoeshine boy and then as a waiter in a restaurant that specialized in paella. In a year, when I had become more certain of my Spanish, I found the courage to present myself at the National Library.

In those years, the library was still directed by Domingo Figarola-Caneda—who was searching for academic guidance. I confess here that I was compelled to misrepresent myself slightly as a doctor of letters from Trinity College. In those years, such claims took time and effort to verify, and so hiring depended much more on character and apparent intelligence than it does now. I don't know if old Domingo saw in me some evidence of genius or whether he simply needed an English-speaker. But whatever the reason, I soon found myself director of a newly created section called Poetry of the Americas. In those years, Cuba was beginning to move away from imperial influences. For some reason, old Domingo saw in this Irishman someone who could purge the library of its foreign mannerisms and replace them with something like Creole honesty. It is given to a few fortunate men the grace to find the perfect intersection between their obsession and their livelihood. So it happened to me, and I have spent the happiest years of my life immersed in Cuban verse. What follows here is a modest anthology of my life's investigations. Modest because, as the reader alone knows, I am not, in fact, a doctor of letters from Trinity College or anywhere else. But I know something of imagination, having sheltered under its enormous shadow-wings. And, though I may not be Cuban, I have learned to speak the language of escape. Untether your expectations; be lifted by these unseen poets struggling to translate that which has no translation. And remember what a great friend once told me: just because it never happened doesn't mean it isn't true.

Herberto Quain
La Habana, 1936

You Are the Heirs of All My Terrors
BY CELESTINO D'ALBA

Many years later, at the end of this story, I found myself, somewhat inexplicably, on a railway platform. It was December. Outside it must have been snowing—I had a memory of snow—but inside the station it was very warm. At first I thought I was alone, but then I realized, with a quickening horror, that I had been joined by two men in long coats. They wore identical black hats and looked like brothers, except one was bearded and the other hairless. Each stood in a puddle of melted ice. They stamped their feet, and every few minutes they moved closer to the rails. The air was humid and menacing.

"He was in a delicate state."

"Yes, very delicate, that's true."

"He couldn't even work anymore."

"And yet, the papers formed an archipelago around his bed."

"But he was drowning on the shore."

"All the same, it is contrary to our policies."

I had a sense the men were talking about me. I stood, listening. I hoped they would say my name, which I had forgotten. How had I arrived here? What was I waiting for? On the other platforms, the trains came and went. Ours alone seemed to be delayed. I thought of searching out a timetable that might give me a clue about my destination, but I was afraid of missing the train. Around me, the men seemed to grow more impatient. But soon other men joined us and they fell into an easy, though hushed, conversation. Over the speakers, a voice in Spanish called out the names of cities that could not possibly connect to this station: Moa. Gibara. Baracoa. The trains had stopped going there years ago. Perhaps this was the cause of the delay. Some-one should tell the stationmaster. But not me; I knew that if I moved from the platform, I would be carried away forever and miss this, my last chance.

Many hours went by. Other passengers joined us. We crowded on the platform now, standing in one another's puddles. I had the feeling that I had been followed here. But the bearded man and the hairless one began to move away. I leaned forward to search for them in the growing crowd. I cocked my ear to their accent—Jesuit-educated, from the east—when a gasp went through the crowd and silenced the station. One man pointed and then others raised their heads. At first I thought a bird was caught in the rafters. But then I saw that it was a child's electric-yellow balloon, its silver string flashing in the shafts of light. The balloon floated and then swooped down on a draft, only to be forced up again higher into the night sky. A train came into the station and the turbulence scattered the balloon across the heavens so that I temporarily lost sight of it. But I soon found it again where the great dome curved down. The others resumed their whispered conversations. But I kept it in my sight. It seemed to be making a tour of the universe, its translucent skin veiling first Aquarius and then Capricorn. At Aries the balloon lingered for a moment and I thought it would rest there until it ran out of helium and floated down to earth. But to my surprise (for the others had long since lost interest in the orphan) the balloon shot from Aries to Pisces, barely missing a prick of the ram, and was sucked up into the void beyond the stars. Never in my life had I seen a balloon penetrate the great skein of heaven. I looked around me to see if someone else had witnessed this extraordinary event. But every man stood with his eyes fixed on the rails.

When next I turned my eyes up, I noticed a breach in the sky, a small black hole near Pisces. The stars were very bright that evening and I thought it a trick of the light and the dome's curvature, until I noticed the balloon's silver string spooling away into nothing. As I watched, a light, like a searchlight, shone through the pinhole in the sky. I followed it to its source, staring up into the hole, and there—there: it could not be, but it was, there in the pinhole of the sky I met an eye staring back at me. The apparition seized my heart with horror enough, but imagine the cold that overtook me when I realized that the eye staring down from heaven was my own. I looked away quickly and then back. The eye still stared, unblinking. It was not the only thing wrong in that hard heaven. For as I stood beneath the dome fixing my stare upon myself, I saw that the stars, the constellations, and the entire firmament were backward, a mirror image, and it was the other eye, the one coolly watching beyond the celestial sphere, that saw things as they were. As the mysteries of this railway station multiplied, I was nearly overcome with anxiety. Where were my bags? Where was I going? Why was the train so delayed? I stood at the platform, wiping my cold wet hands on my trousers. I bowed my head from heaven; there was nothing but confusion there. The important thing was to make the train. I waited for what seemed hours, maybe days, but my legs did not grow tired. The sun never rose—inside it was always night, the platform glowing in the electric light of those perverse stars. Around midnight of what could have been the third day, a cry went up on the platform. Then a hush—the rails hummed softly. A train approached! We were now packed elbow to elbow on the platform. There would not be room for all of us on the train. I was carried along in the crush to the platform's edge. As I struggled to gain footing, the two men in overcoats reappeared. They were pushing their way through the crowd with ease, pointing at me. The hairless one smiled, as if he were a friend who only wanted to say hello. But the bearded one scowled as he shoved away everyone in his path. I knew I must get away. I must run. The announcer cried out a destination. So this was it, the last train to Cojimar. I remembered now that it had been my wish to take in the sun one last time, to cover again the leaves in verse. I knew I must force my legs to move. But the men in overcoats were gaining; they were bigger and faster while I was weak and ill. Worse, the waiting men seemed to be on their side. Soon all were pointing me out for my killers as I ducked and tried to slip through the crowd. In the distance, a train whistle blew. The great eye—my own traitorous eye—regarded me from heaven, with neither pity nor interest. The rails hummed. I felt rough hands on me. The men in overcoats closed in as the others held me fast, an offering. I spun free of my coat and ran, feeling light now, so light that I nearly leapt through the outstretched hands before me, all trace of illness gone with my soiled coat. I braced for impact. With a great concussion of air, the train swept into the station, bearing with it the smell of the sea.

Cojimar
BY ERNESTO DEL CAMINO

Everything about him was old except his eyes and they were the same color as the sea. He had stopped fishing years ago, but he had not stopped coming to the beach. In his day it had been only about the fishing. The rocky shore covered in skiffs. Now it was different. The fish had disappeared, and the beach was for leaving. He stood on the deck of La Terraza, next to Papa's bronze head, and stared out over the shore. Not yet seven A.M. and already they were gathering.

Earlier that morning, in a different city, the boy was woken by his mother. That's how it is for children: they are always being acted upon. They are woken and fed and they are walked to school, where they are then, for eight long hours, taught how to be. Children are slaves of other voices. They have not yet mastered the first person singular and are always at the blunt end of someone else's dream.

So the boy was woken early that morning by his mother, whom he, naturally, adored. She was his sun and his moon, his waking and his sleeping. And that Monday morning in November when she shook him awake, her face was the first thing he saw, luminous in the wan light of early morning. Or, as he would have said it had we given him the chance to speak: her face looked pretty and soft in the dark. She smelled of soap.

And when she kissed him, he reached up with his thin arms to hang on her neck.

She told him to hurry, that the others were waiting. And school? No school. Later, in Miami. Miami. People were always talking about Miami. He had asked his father about it. They were standing outside together beneath a mango tree that had not given fruit that year. His father had turned him to face the smell of the ocean and pointed up, through the leaves. "Miami is that way."

So Miami was someplace in the sky, behind the clouds. Curious. If he had religious training, he might have thought Miami was in heaven, with Papa Dios. His mother thought that and so did many others. But he didn't know about things like heaven or God. Miami was just a cloud city beyond sight. Someplace that hovered over the waters and that's where they were going. They were going on a ship. His mother had told him all about it, preparing. And when he asked how they would get to the clouds, she had laughed.

The boy and his mother lived in Matanzas, a province in Cuba that writers love because it means "the killings," and it gives them a chance to comment on how bloody this bloody awful land is. And it's true. If it were in a book, you couldn't say the boy lived in Matanzas because it would be too ridiculous. But he did. Truth is the strangest thing you'll ever know.

That morning, though, the morning the boy was awakened before dawn, Matanzas was at peace. The only sound was of roosters crowing in the distance, and the air through the open windows was cool and nice. He was happy and snuggled closer to his mother. Don't go back to sleep, son. You need to get dressed. She was warm, so warm. Hurry, boy, hurry.

A man he didn't know picked them up by the monument to the bicycle in Cárdenas. His mother thought this was funny. We're going to pedal all the way to Miami, she said. There were already others in the truck, each of them holding a small bundle. They laughed also. The boy knew some of them. He worried that the ship would be too heavy with all these people, and they would not be able to lift into the clouds. He wanted to tug at his mother to tell her, but he didn't want her to laugh at him again in front of the others. So he leaned against her thigh and closed his eyes as the truck bumped along the empty road in the dark.

It was still dark when they arrived in Cojimar. Others had arrived before them. Some were taking their coffee at La Terraza, which every morning opened earlier and earlier. It had once been a famous bar for the tourists: its black bean soup had been featured in a European travel guide, and for six months La Terraza had more Spanish and Dutch backpackers than it could feed. These days, though, most of the traffic was in the curious and the foolhardy.

The old man stood on the deck and nodded at the boy and his mother. The mother ordered water, saying it was for the boy, but the old man understood and made her a coffee as well. He brought the boy a guava pastry. When the mother said she didn't have money, the old man held up his hand.

"I have my own," he said. "I know."

The boy thanked him, but did not eat the pastry. The old man looked at the boy and then at the mother.

"He is young," the old man said.

"Six, almost seven," said the mother. "He is small for his age."

"Too small for that long journey," the old man said. He saw something in the boy's eyes.

"We are only going fishing," the mother said.

"All the same, the boy is young and fragile and the sea is deep and rough."

"It is a short fishing trip," the woman said, pulling the boy close to her. "Don't bring the evil eye down on us."

"Go with God," the old man said.

At the water's edge, the boy had tried to run back. No, no, no, that ship cannot fly! The others laughing. The boy hated these kinds of jokes that he couldn't understand. The boy had almost reached La Terraza. The old man, watching, took a step down onto the rocky beach. But one of the men from the raft caught up with the boy and held him aloft. His legs kicked and the old man thought he looked like a sad little crab.

"That ship cannot fly!" the boy screamed into the sky.

The old man realized that the boy could not swim. He took another step toward the shore, but the man already had the boy on the raft. Twice, the boy tried to jump out and a crowd from La Terraza gathered to watch.

"Shameful."

"What some people do for money."

"Endanger yourself if you want, but don't be selfish with the children."

"Look there! He's jumped out."

"That poor boy."

"The boy has jumped."

The old man did not see this, but the raft was too far out now for him to be able to count its passengers. Besides, he could not remember how many had boarded on the shore.

Dawn had come, but brought with it little light. The sky was low and gray. The sea was dark. A few young men swam out, but they were turned back by the waves. For a while it seemed there would be no more launchings, but after an hour, the first raft went out into the rough sea. And then another and another. They had come this far. And if others judged it safe . . .

The old man spent the rest of the morning writing down orders in his notebook and watching out over the sea. In the afternoon, the clouds shifted inland. The sea calmed. The old man was taking an order for black beans when the second shout went out.

Body in the surf!

The old man put his pad and pen in his pocket and hurried down to the shore. He was old and did not move quickly. So by the time he got to the water's edge, a crowd had already gathered. He strained to see past them. In the water, about twenty meters out, something dark moved and bobbed. The boy, the old man said quietly. The boy jumped.

Some men were already in the water. The strongest of them swam almost to the body, but was pushed back by the current. He returned to the shore, panting. I saw the body; it's the boy. A shout went up: A boat, a boat! The young men ran to the harbor to ask for help. Only the old man stayed behind. He waited, watching the dark bobbing and knowing that all was already lost. The others were a long time returning. Later, it emerged that the police would not grant them a rescue boat—the illegal activities of Cojimar being well documented by the indifferent but cruel authority. But it was just as well. For as the old man waited on the shore, the current brought the body closer and closer. The man waded in to his knees to receive it. It had been many years since he had felt the sting of seawater, and the sensation took him back to his youth. With what vitality he had met life, with what hope he had pushed out every morning from the shore, the stars still brilliant in the firmament!

One last wave carried the body high and, in retreating, laid it on the sand. The old man pushed out of the water as quickly as he could. The body lay sideways on the shore, its highest point rising and falling as with breath. The man's heart caught in his throat.

Now he was running to the body that was not, in fact, a body. My Lord, the old man said. For at his feet, tangled with seaweed and moss, was a giant jellyfish, the likes of which had never been seen in Cojimar. It was almost exactly the size of a small boy caught inside a balloon. Its iridescent yellow body expanded and contracted in the breeze. The man watched it for a moment. The others were fast approaching. He had only a moment. The old man felt in his pocket for the pen. He mumbled an old prayer. And in one swift stroke all that was left of the jellyfish was a withered yellow film, which the next wave carried back out to sea.

The Boy Who Was Rescued by Fish
BY TERESA DE LA LANDRE

For reasons that are too complicated to get into, it had been a trying month at the organization and Beatrice, our leader, finally called a meeting at La Carreta.

"I want to start a new era," she said. "An era of hope, of positive thoughts, of good things." We feared what was coming. Beatrice once fired a new girl when she found a homemade Eleguá in her drawer. The organization, Beatrice warned, had a zero-tolerance policy for Santería. Eleguá, Yemayá, and Santa Bárbara (unless it was thundering) were spirits non grata in this office so long as Beatrice was boss. But for all that, Beatrice was a fundamentalist believer in American Santería, the branch of religion that includes crystals, self-help, and sprouted pumpkin seeds. "Positive thoughts?" said Lucy. She could not suppress a sigh. Mia, as ever, sat hunched next to Beatrice like a giant crane, nodding at every other word. Beatrice ignored them both and plowed ahead, a breezy smile on her lips.

"Ladies, I want to introduce you to our salvation," Beatrice said. She reached into her purse and pulled out a book.

"A book?" said Lucy. "We're going to be saved by a book?"

"Not just any book," said Beatrice, smiling. "*The Undisclosed.*"

"The undisclosed what?" said Lucy.

"Just *The Undisclosed*," I said. "It's a self-help book that's all the rage. I can't believe you've never heard of it."

Lucy shrugged. "I don't watch television," she said.

"It is not a 'self-help book,' Zenia," said Beatrice, making quotation marks in the air. "It is a serious book full of wisdom known to sages since the time of Moses."

"OK," I said.

Mia looked at me. You could say, in the style of some books, that she shot me a disapproving glance.

"I read it straight through in one sitting," Beatrice said. "And then I read it again." She nodded at Mia, who, taking her cue, took three copies of the book out of her bag. "I've bought each of you a copy and I want you to study it. It has changed my life and it will change yours. Together, we will change ours," Beatrice said.

She stared at us, waiting. No one spoke. So she continued. "It seems like such a simple prescription, and yet it's so profound: change your thinking and you will change your life."

Lucy closed her eyes and put her fingers to her forehead. "I'm thinking that I'm going to win a million dollars and have enough money to pay for a nurse for my husband." She opened her eyes and smiled mildly.

"It doesn't work like that," said Beatrice. "You can't be sarcastic. You have to really believe it. You have to ask the universe for what you want and then know that it will come to you. The universe will take care of you, but it doesn't like sarcasm."

"I've been warned," said Lucy.

She turned to me and smiled. I really had nothing to say. Honestly, I had no opinion one way or another on *The Undisclosed*. But I sensed that my job was on the line. At least I should seem curious. Beatrice liked curiosity. On the other hand, I liked Lucy, too. I tried to respond in a way that would please them both.

"How is this different from . . ." I almost said "Santería," but not wanting to antagonize Beatrice, I just said, "religion? You know, praying?"

"I'm glad you asked," said Beatrice, who had now settled comfortably into her role as chief educator and pronouncer. "Religion posits a single unknowable God whom one must worship and bribe and plead with."

"Also saints," added Lucy, but Beatrice ignored her.

"*The Undisclosed* is not about that; it's not about an entity; it's much more mystical, much more all-encompassing," Beatrice said. "It's all about the law of magnets. You know, the way magnets attract other magnets and iron things. I can't explain it as well as the book; that's why I want you to read it. This lady knows her stuff."

"For sure. Look at all the success she's had with the book," I said. I meant it to affirm Beatrice's general thesis, but when Lucy laughed I realized the way it had come out. Beatrice pursed her lips at me. But in keeping with her new positivism, she didn't call me out.

"There are negative energies and positive energies in the world, ladies," she said, continuing. "No one can deny that. Don't you ever experience that tingling feeling on the back of your neck when a certain person walks into a room?"

She held her hand up: "Stop that thought," she said. "Don't focus on a particular person. Don't focus on that negative experience. I just want to illustrate for you that negative and positive are at work in the universe and we can choose to tap into one or the other."

"So the idea is to become tyrants of our own thoughts," Lucy said.

Beatrice finally turned the full force of her body toward Lucy.

"You are my dearest friend, Lucy, and I want the best, the most happiness for you," she said. "That's why I beg you to let go of this negative outlook of yours, this unhealthy skepticism that is poisoning your life."

Lucy frowned.

Beatrice turned to address the rest of us. "After I read this book, I completely understood what's wrong with us Cubans. We focus on the negative, on hate, on revenge. We constantly use words like Tyrant, Dictator, Dungeon. We have dedicated our energies to thinking and living and breathing . . . That Man!"

She opened her eyes wide. "Our thoughts have kept him in power, have nourished him, have expanded the negative vibe that gives him strength. Our thoughts, ladies, have been a yeast to his evil."

The boy who had been picking up our coffee cups at that moment stopped in midair. We all stared at Beatrice.

"What?"

"A yeast?"

I cleared my throat, and this seemed to break the spell. The boy kept moving, Lucy coughed lightly. Mia leaned back against the booth.

"So," I said, trying to steer the topic away from bread-making, "if we had just been thinking good and happy thoughts, we wouldn't be getting audited?"

The barest frown crossed Beatrice's face. I had introduced a negative ion. But she let it go. "It's not quite like that," Beatrice said. "It's not so simple. But something in us, as an organization, has become unbalanced, maybe. And this has—temporarily—shifted the forces of the universe against us."

She took a sip of water and brushed back her hair. "Then there are the negative thoughts of others," she said—a little ominously, if you ask me. "People can wish you harm and if their thoughts are stronger than yours . . . But no talk of this! No talk of negative thoughts, no negative thinking!"

Lucy raised her eyebrows and took a deep sigh. "It's an interesting theory," she said finally. "I'll try to put it to work."

This seemed to please Beatrice even more. She ordered a tres leches and asked for the bill. "It's all going to work out for us," she said. "I'm positive."

~

So, in addition to our work promoting freedom and democracy in Cuba, as well as fending off the GAO auditors, we now had to cram for the positive-thinking exams.

Over the next few days, Beatrice embarked on a wide-ranging revolution that included some light redecorating. She pushed our single bit of art—an oil painting of Varadero beach—into the hallway that led to her office, and, in her words, cleansed and brightened up the communal work space. Now, the walls in the main wing were covered with posters of animals offering uplifting advice.

"Hang in there," admonished a monkey doing just that in some tropical forest.

"Believe," said a whale, obscurely.

A half-buried ostrich said, presumably in a muffled voice, "It will get better."

Lucy added her own wisdom, declaring in a serious voice, "When you live in a zoo, you get used to the stink." But the rest of us kept our counsel. It was unsettling to see Beatrice in those weeks. She laughed, she hummed, she bought us pastries. In other words, she was not in any way herself.

The Beatrice I had always known was a strong lady, given to kooky beliefs, it's true, but unsparing in her ambition. She had single-handedly founded the Cuban American National Treasury after a falling-out with the better-known foundation down the street. She was tough-minded and very quotable, and for the last ten years CANT, with her at the helm, had added much to the Cuba debate in Miami. I'd come to work here right after college, and though I was looking for a way out, perhaps into private industry, for now CANT was all I had. Not that I minded it. My job as media liaison was to promote the need for a Free and Democratic Cuba, not a hard task in a town where everyone pretty much agrees on the need for a Free and Democratic Cuba. Problem was, the last month had been a bit rocky. Like other organizations dedicated to a Free and Democratic Cuba, CANT received most of its funds through USAID. Now, thanks to the socialists who had come to power in Washington, some of our expenditures had come into question. Why, the auditors at the GAO wanted to know, did we purchase $53,000 worth of Godiva chocolates in 1995? This was so insulting. As if the children of Cuba didn't deserve the finest chocolates and instead should be forced to make do with the insipid and chalky garbage produced by Hershey's. But it was pointless to argue with the GAO and we certainly weren't going to take our fight public with the local newspaper, which we all called *The Horror*. So there was nothing to do but lie low, cooperate as much as possible, think positive thoughts, and hope that the auditors didn't find the purchase of four fur coats from Macy's in January 1997 (company trip to New York).

Given all we were going through, the part about thinking only positive thoughts seemed the easiest. Even Lucy got into it, I believe. And by the end of that month, there was a perceptible change in the office.

"Good day, Lucy," I said.

"Beautiful, isn't it?"

Her psoriasis, Lucy reported, had cleared up. And her husband, while not improving, at least seemed to be getting no worse.

The changes were even more pronounced in Beatrice, probably because she was the one who had the most faith in the system. She looked simply radiant, and may have even lost some weight. Mia is not even worth mentioning; whatever Beatrice was, so was she. For all I know, Mia might have been one of those holograms everyone was talking about.

So we ambled along, awash in affirmations. And then a truly remarkable thing happened, for which we could really only credit *The Undisclosed*, and the power of the combined positive energy of the CANT office: a news event so big, so momentous, so life-altering that it pushed the silly issues with the GAO right off the front page.

~

The story broke on a Saturday. A raft had been spotted off Key West overnight. Of the twelve men, women, and children on board, there had been only one survivor: a boy of six, small for his age. Even more miraculously, the boy had been kept alive by dolphins, a fact confirmed by fishermen who, just before plucking the boy from the sea, had seen the animals frolicking near him.

Monday, as you might imagine, was a joyous day in the CANT offices, as it was across Miami. Beatrice called another meeting at La Carreta. We ordered the usual—vaca frita—and got down to business.

"Some of you may not be aware of this," Beatrice began. "But we are living in the Age of Pisces. I repeat, the Age of

Pisces. Not, as the hippie song had it, the Age of Aquarius. I don't know where they got that nonsense when anyone can see that the vernal equinox is still in Pisces. In fact, we entered the Age of Pisces after the fall of Rome and will remain in it for another five hundred years."

"That's a relief," said Lucy. "Maybe we should have ordered the fish."

Beatrice ignored her. "The Age of Pisces is also called the Age of Spirituality. It is the age that gave rise to the great monotheistic religions of the world, and it is during this age that mankind has felt the urge to transcend the boundaries of the physical world. Think flight, think rocket science, think a little boy rescued by fish!"

We all clapped. Beatrice was convinced that our positive thoughts had brought not just our own salvation but that of the boy. And she became obsessed with the story—even more so than the rest of Miami, which is saying a lot.

Indeed, as the silly audit story vanished from the front pages, Beatrice became more and more involved in the case of the Little Pisces, as she came to nickname the unfortunate boy. This was fine for a while. And I didn't mind the daily lectures on astrology. It was pretty cool, actually, to learn that Pisces represented another, very ancient, mother-son escape.

"When Aphrodite and her son Eros were harassed and pursued by the dictator Typhon," Beatrice explained, "they turned themselves into two fish and set off for the great ocean of the cosmos, their mighty escape recorded for all time in our heavens."

"Is that so?" said Lucy.

Beatrice didn't believe in coincidences. Everything in the universe fitted together, like a cosmic puzzle. And this miracle boy, rescued by fishes after a daring escape with his mother under the protection of Pisces, could mean only one thing: divinity.

I could go with this. I'd had a loose, mediocre education that afforded me just enough of the liberal arts to be sufficiently open to whatever. But after a few weeks, Beatrice's mania put a not inconsiderable strain on the day-to-day running of the office.

Plus, the Little Pisces was beginning to grate. What had begun as a heartwarming story of a rescue soon ballooned into an unwieldy drama of international intrigue, ruined reputations, and general madness. Soon, Beatrice was neglecting the work of a Free and Democratic Cuba altogether, instead spending her time taking part in marches, signing petitions, and attending all-night prayer vigils at the home of the boy's relatives, with whom, Beatrice believed, God himself wished the boy to remain.

That meant more work for me. Not that I wasn't sympathetic to the plight of the boy. Don't think me so self-absorbed that I could not feel for the poor child, who had lost his mother and probably his entire sense of security on that crossing. I also understood that we were living through a very important moment in the history of Miami.

But it was pretty unfair of Beatrice to decamp and leave the detailed work of CANT—press releases, interviews, and other minutiae—to us. Plus, though the paper had dropped the story, there was still the fine point of the GAO audit, which continued.

And guess who had to do the heavy lifting with the auditors. I was strung out and grouchy. But when I complained to Beatrice about the impossible workload, she told me to "think positive." Two days later, she ordered all of us to go through our desktop dictionaries and cut out the word "impossible."

Not cool. Unlike Lucy, I had read *The Undisclosed* from cover to cover. And I was truly trying to put its teachings into practice. For example, one day, I walked into a door and broke my little toe. "Thank goodness," I forced myself to say to myself, "that it wasn't more serious." When my pressure cooker blew up, spewing chícharos all over the ceiling, I told everyone how lucky it was that I had been far away from the kitchen when it happened. (Lucy, of course, had to suggest that my being far from the kitchen was the reason it exploded in the first place.) My cubicle was now papered with happy things: photos of my niece and nephew, yellow smiley faces, kittens, sunsets. I'd even hung up the serenity prayer that Beatrice gave us, along with a collection of her favorite uplifting sayings. (At the top of the list: "Become a possibilitarian!") But after a few weeks of this, I found myself glummer and glummer. It wasn't just me. Beatrice's happy face had taken on a waxy sheen. Mia seemed to have gone mute with joy. I worried most about Lucy, whose smile looked so forced now that some days it seemed closer to a grimace. For my part, the strain was mostly mental. I found myself constantly policing my thoughts and worrying endlessly should a stray negative idea insinuate itself into my happy fortress. I worried about getting sick, and then I'd worry about being worried and about even introducing the word "sick" into my mental processes and thus putting it out into the universe, like a big attractive neon sign: SICK—COME TO ME, BABY.

My thoughts about the Little Pisces were the worst. The kid, at least in the snippets I caught on the news, looked miserable, though you could not actually say this, not in Miami and certainly not within earshot of the Positive Police. But just thinking it made me worry that I would attract the forces of misery to him. And that was the last thing he needed. The boy needed positive thoughts, especially since the socialist government in Washington had gotten involved and was talking of "reuniting" the boy with his father, who had, against all common sense, elected to stay in Cuba.

These were trying times in Miami. Many friendships collapsed. In the CANT offices, we tried to keep a happy face on things, even as it became clear that the Little Pisces might actually be sent back to Cuba.

Meanwhile, Beatrice had moved to the forefront of the movement to save the boy. She wrote bright, optimistic editorials that *The Horror* was finally happy to publish. She went on the radio. She camped overnight at Chez Little Pisces. She was a constant—ebullient, smiling—presence at the prayer vigils held there every Thursday night.

One day, the thing I had been fearing (and desperately trying to push out of my mind) finally came to pass: Beatrice asked me to join her. I told her that I wasn't quite ready, that I was still working on cultivating the proper possibilitarianism, that I feared my propensity to dark thoughts (weirdly magnified since the positive campaign) would harm the boy. Beatrice would have none of that. She was positive enough for the two of us, she assured me. She was a veritable force field of happiness, a high dam against darkness, the defender of the constant, maddening smile.

The crappy house was set among other crappy houses in a crappy neighborhood. I tried not to think of this, tried not to concentrate on the crappiness and instead notice the sunshine and how beautiful the fluffy clouds were, how they flitted across the sky.

"Don't forget the singing birds," Beatrice said.

And the singing birds, of course. Lovely so long as one remained out of their line of fire. My God, I just couldn't help it. I wished that I could turn off my brain. But of course, the more I wished it, the more elusive any kind of control became. I was under a lot of stress, truth be told. And the circumstances at Chez Little Pisces did not help.

All was chaos. Do you know that scene in *La Dolce Vita* when Marcello and his nutjob girlfriend go to the countryside to check out the Virgin Mary? The mobs, the lights, the rain, the con artists? That's what it was like here. The place was crawling with overweight, leering cameramen and anorexic women draped in telegenic colors. The news trucks spewed their diesel so that you could hardly breathe within a mile radius of the cursed place. And the klieg lights or whatever they were called now turned the whole thing into a stage, a twenty-four-hour daylight extravaganza to be processed, packaged, and resold to an unsuspecting gringo population that could only think, *What The Fuck*? In short, the scene was a total nightmare and nothing at all conducive to the cultivation of positive thoughts.

In the midst of all this, Beatrice amazed me. True, her face these days sometimes seemed to be unnaturally and painfully pinched. But her voice was light and seductive, her smile curiously radiant. Everyone wanted to talk to her, and everyone, it seemed, knew her.

"The Beatific One!" yelled a man from across the street.

Beatrice waved over to him and threw him a kiss.

"We are going to win, my lovely!"

"We are indeed," Beatrice yelled back. "Stay positive."

In reply, the man punched a fist in the air.

Beatrice took my elbow and, like an old expert, maneuvered me around the crowd. I couldn't tell what time it was. It could have been noon or midnight, though it was probably closer to dinnertime given that most of the camera crews were now crouching around their trucks like members of some gross urban animal pack, scooping up food from plastic containers.

I followed Beatrice up the street and to the front lawn, where two big men opened the chain-link fence to let us in. I had begun to sweat. I tried to concentrate on flowers, birds, freedom, health, prosperity. "I will be a possibilitarian," I said silently to myself. "I am strong. I am a positive person. I am a lovable child of the universe and deserve all the good things that mother cosmos has to offer me."

Before I knew it, Beatrice was standing on a homemade-looking plywood platform and a group of us were surrounding her, hand in hand. My back was to the street and I was forced to face that sad little house. Its pale-green paint was peeling, the wood frame around the door rotting. The curtains on the windows were firmly shut, though now and then they seemed to move as in a breeze. I tried, but could not construct a positive frame for any of this.

"Brothers and sisters," Beatrice began. "We must join our good thoughts, our mercy, our positivism so that the universe may take note of our goodness and grant that the Little Pisces remain among us here in freedom's lap as his dear mother intended."

"Amen," called the woman next to me. Her hand was puffed and damp, but each time I made as if to release it, she clamped down harder.

"Pisces can be an inconstant sign, my friends. Born in conflict, peril, and escape, it has a future as unstable as its past," Beatrice continued. "But the fish is a wily and agile creature, ever swimming toward freedom, ever seeking the deep ocean of the soul, the transcendence of imagination. Let us now draw up a mental image of the fish that saved the Little Pisces. Concentrate your thoughts on their selflessness, their playfulness. Meditate on the bottomless well of goodness that steered them to the boy and proved his salvation. Let us be equal to their sacrifice and bounty."

"Amen," the others repeated. More punishing lights blazed behind me, and I was glad that my back was to the crowd.

But it wasn't over. Beatrice spoke for almost an hour, exhorting the faithful to "banish negative thoughts" and warning them that "we will get the outcome we expect, so we should expect victory." Maybe it was the harsh lights, but Beatrice's face did not look good. Deep furrows had set along her mouth, and her cheerful countenance seemed to have collapsed into a gray pallor. Given all this, her permanent smile had suddenly acquired a demented quality. It was hard to look at her for very long now without shuddering. I soon found my eyes wandering. Our handholding circle consisted of about fifteen people, all but one of them women. Now and then one of them would shout "Amen!" or "Power to the Positive!" Rosaries dangled from clasped hands. The house before me seemed abandoned, still. At the beginning of Beatrice's talk, I had half-expected the front door to open and one of the Little Pisces's relatives to come out and join us or else tell us to get the hell off their beaten lawn. Nothing of the sort happened. But as Beatrice was winding down ("And so, my brothers and sisters . . .") a slight movement caught my eye, a flutter in the curtains. And as I stared, the curtains parted ever so slightly and a little face peered out. Big brown eyes seemed to scan that loopy landscape for a moment—terrified—before a pair of big hands drew the curtains violently closed.

~

They took him away a week later. The news hit the CANT offices like a great big bucketful of "no." Beatrice didn't even show up until late afternoon, her powdered face streaked with the most negative tears. She locked herself in her office and wouldn't speak to anyone. I guess she was as sorry about the boy's return as she was about the utter collapse of the teachings of *The Undisclosed*.

For my part (though I would never admit this publicly and have kept it to myself these many years) the return of the Little Pisces was one of my life's most joyous moments, like a fever breaking, a great unburdening, a reprieve from the land of yes. I have seen tiny spiders crawl to the edge of a twig, spin out their delicate silk threads, and launch themselves into the wind. That's how I felt.

About a month after the boy's return, Beatrice called another meeting at La Carreta. Her serious face was pink and healthy. We ordered the dolphin and ate like cannibals. And then Beatrice got down to business, laying out her plans for responding to the GAO audit.

"We will commence our attack tomorrow morning," she began. "I have already booked radio time. Mia, you will come with me. Lucy, you will go on *Osman Hasa* Thursday night; I've already arranged everything. Wear the leopard print. Zenia, you will draw up our talking points, and next week I've scheduled a lunch for you with the editorial director of *The Horror*." She smiled, genuinely, peacefully, and brought her hands together as if in prayer.

"No mercy, ladies," she said. "We will destroy them."

The Boy's Triumphant Return

LA HABANA—Today a miraculous and heroic sight: a kidnapped Cuban boy returned triumphantly to the fatherland on a jet that soared over the clear skies of the capital, passing once, twice like a bird before nimbly landing on native soil. In its belly: the little hero who had been ruthlessly and illegally held in Miami since being kidnapped last November by his mother and forced aboard a raft across the Straits. Of the fifteen criminals trying to flee to North America, only the boy survived, rescued by fishermen. Now, finally, our long nightmare has come to an end and we welcome the bright tomorrow that dawns.

Our fatherland has reached an honorable and just victory, after seven months of energized, indefatigable, intelligent, and decisive struggle, with the liberation and the return to Cuba of the kidnapped child next to his dignified and valiant father. This battle that we are prepared to wage to the ultimate consequences demonstrated the unity, the firmness, the heroism, and the thirst for struggle of our valiant nation.

It is necessary to continue, without losing one moment, without giving space to fatigue, until we eliminate the causes that gave rise to this tragedy. It is imperative that we do everything necessary to prevent a repetition, and that is the only thing that will succeed in devastating the criminal migratory politics that have been deliberately conceived to destabilize and undermine Cuban society, cynically calculated to provoke deaths and suffering, shamelessly manipulating the tragedies occasioned by this law.

In Defense of Flying
by Carla Gades

Today I went flying over a cypress forest near my house. It was almost sunset and cool, the air scented, and it struck me, not for the first time, that I was alone in the sky.

I have been flying for almost twenty years, and cannot now imagine a life without flight. It began for me, as I suppose it does for all fliers, with a crisis. The details of the crisis are of no concern to anyone anymore, but it is enough to say, I think, that I discovered all those years ago that there was no finer way to ease the mind than to open the door to the outside, find a good stretch of road to get a good running speed going, and then—lift up, up, up, away from the hard ground. Even after all these years, those first few moments of flight bring me immeasurable joy, and writing about it now fills every bone in my wings with an electric anticipation that is a kind of ecstasy. I am well aware that most people become embarrassed by this sort of talk. So I try, when working to persuade someone to take up flying, to concentrate (at least at first) on the medical benefits. These are well-known to anyone who reads the literature (see, in particular, "Flying Seen to Have Positive Effects on the Heart," from the *Wisconsin Quarterly Medical Review* (September 1999); and "Endorphins and Nonimpact Sports," from *Psychology Today* (May 2002). Flying, as studies have shown over the years, helps keep weight down (a pressing issue in our day), helps control cholesterol, and staves off the muscle loss that is responsible for many of the aches and pains of growing old. But the benefits are not only physical. We know that flying releases the feel–good chemicals in the brain that help stabilize mood in patients suffering everything from depression to migraine headaches.

So why do so few people fly? It's a question that has long perplexed me. I remember when I first started flying seriously—every day after school. My aunt, with whom I was living at the time, warned me that flight was bad for women. The sudden burst of speed needed to get off the ground, combined with the weightlessness of prolonged flight, she argued, could make my ovaries become detached and fall. It goes without saying that there is absolutely no medical basis for this assertion. When I persisted in my flight training, she and my cousin both told me that only tomboys flew. They warned me that the constant flapping needed for flying would overdevelop the muscles of my forewings and ruin the "feminine" contours of my body. This, I knew even then, was ludicrous. If women are able to develop muscles, then muscles are just as "feminine" as anything else we can do with our bodies. Or is "feminine" to be a synonym for "atrophy"? Still, I was very young then and the constant criticism did hurt my confidence. I even stopped flying for a few months, as I remember, though I promptly took it up again when I saw that it was the best way to process the daily challenges of my life. I can imagine that these conversations still go on in dining rooms all across this country. And perhaps they are to blame for the fact that among fliers, who are few to begin with, women are very poorly represented. Another thing that I hear a lot is, "You're going to ruin your elbows" or "The ulna and radius weren't designed to withstand so much constant motion." Designed? I prefer to think of it as "developed." But just the same, let's say we follow the design argument: why would we have been given wings if we weren't meant to use them? As for the ulna and the radius, they are very strong bones, evolved over many millennia to function efficiently. I would argue that not to use them regularly goes against our very nature. As Edward O. Wilson said many times, we evolved for this planet, not any other.

I'm not always alone up there, it's true. Every spring, when the weather turns lovely, new fliers will join me in wheels above the forest (which is the nicest place for flying where I live; during the migrating season, you can even find yourself flying next to giant flocks of geese). Some of the new fliers are a sight—their bodies awkward and slow. It's a wonder some of them can even get off the ground. Still, I always smile and wave when I fly past them, by way of encouragement. But come summer, the numbers begin to dwindle. And by the time school starts again in the fall, I'm up there by myself again.

People get discouraged. I can't blame them. Flying can be exhausting, especially if it's done without joy. That's why it's a pleasure to see children, who jump and run and fly without any self-consciousness, without even a thought to whether what they do is good or bad or tiring or serves any purpose whatsoever. What happens? When do we lose that beautiful recklessness?

I shudder to see the way so many people lead their lives, without color or hope. They get up in the morning, they go to work, they come home, they watch television. Some of them get on the computer for hours. Some even play video games—many of which include complicated digital images of people flying! Only in their dreams, it seems, are people truly free. It occurs to me that if we couldn't fly we'd pine after flying, watching birds wheeling in the sky. We might even dream of it, the way people dream of swimming, as a kind of living experience that evolution denied us. How often have I been at a party and people will start to talk about their dreams of swimming and how they wish to move through the water like fish. And I want to say to them, "But you can fly, and so few of you do!" People dream of swimming only because they can't do it. If man could swim, only about five percent would do it regularly anyway. Swimming, like flying, would tire the muscles. People would need to find time in the day to do it. Some would be afraid of fish, the way they are of birds. Others would complain of getting wet. But people instead think, What a pity that our bodies cannot float. . . .

Of all the arguments against regular flying that I have to endure, the one that really makes me angry is the appeal to moderation. People ask, Must you fly every day? My own mother used to scold me, warning me about a need for "balance" and suggesting that I was perhaps "addicted." To these people, life is to be measured out in spoonfuls, and all of it in proper proportions. What a joyless way to live! Would we say to the young man in love with his girl: Now look, be moderate in your affections. Think about her now and then, but not too often. Remember a proper life consists of time for work and time for play and another, separate, time for love. Don't spend all your time showing her you love her; have her understand that a man's life is hard, and that for much of your life you will have to be apart from her. . . . Such advice might make for a very successful man, but love for him is finished. Better to be like Goethe, who wrote, unashamedly, with all the exuberance and faith of youth, "Oh, how often I used to yearn in those days to fly with wings of the crane above me to the shores of the limitless and drink the surging joy of life from the foaming cup of eternity and feel, with the restricted powers of my breast, one single drop of the bliss of Him who created all this."

The thing is that flying is what the Epicureans would have called a difficult pleasure. Watching television is an easy pleasure; it exerts no muscles, makes no demands on our intelligence, and it requires no special effort. Neither does it bring exceptional joy. In fact, I would argue, the extreme passivity dulls our capacity for true enjoyment. Flying, it is true, requires some effort. But, oh, the rewards! I think now of Montaigne, who wrote that flying consoled him and relieved him of idleness, that it blunted the stabs of pain and distracted him from morose thoughts. I am not trying to say that flying is a cure for everything that ails us. The human being is more complex than that. All I'm suggesting is that we have within both our bodies and our minds an almost infinite capacity to observe and derive pleasure from the world in which we find ourselves. But so few people develop these capacities to the full. Flying is just one small example, and, if I am honest, the only one that I am equipped to speak about with any authority. Still, anyone can see that there are many more examples of the kind, an almost embarrassing assortment of ways to blunt our progress through life. (Surely you, reading this so carefully, following even the demands to stop and read inside the parentheses, would agree with me. Perhaps you're even thinking of an example or two of your own. Or perhaps you disagree entirely, believing like Schopenhauer that we can regard our life as a uselessly disturbing episode in the blissful repose of nothingness. Well, then, I am sorry for you. My goal in this piece is not to change anyone's opinion, really. I just want to open the discussion. But I'm well aware that by a certain age, each man and woman has arrived at a handful of truths that they then begin to constrain their lives by. So be it. Il vaut mieux laisser les hommes pour ce qu'ils sont, que les prendre pour ce qu'ils ne sont pas.)

Of course there is suffering. Of course the purpose of life is not merely to seek pleasure for oneself. But tell me, how does watching television three hours a night decrease the suffering of the world? Wouldn't that time be better spent outdoors, developing our physical selves and deriving a sense of our place in the heavens?

Perhaps I am straying too far from the thesis of this piece, which, as I envisioned it, was really quite simple: to promote more flying. These are just some of the things that I think about when I'm up there alone, no fliers for miles, just me and the air above me and the air beneath me and the earth below crowded with little cars and little houses where now and then I catch the outline of my shadow-wings.

Glossary of Caribbean Winds
BY VIETOR FÚKA

Blow, winds, and crack your cheeks! rage! blow!
—William Shakespeare, *King Lear*

Aeolian: A west wind that begins to blow off the Sierra Maestra when anyone, but especially a husband, begins to plan for a long journey.

Bayamo: A very violent wind born, like many poets, in the Bight of Bayamo. It often vanishes as quickly as it came, but sometimes can persist for years, impeding those who wish to return quickly home.

Boreas: This is the name given to the violent north wind that blows in the early winter mornings. The wind arises in the foothills above Cienfuegos and sweeps out to sea with great force. In ancient times, this wind was said to have sunk four hundred ships in the bay of Cienfuegos. More recently, it has been observed sweeping snakes, grain, and even horses out to sea.

Brisa: The cooling northeast wind that blows throughout the Caribbean to accompany the trade winds. It is called a **brisote** when it blows with unusual force, turning the thoughts of those who are caught in it to foreign lands.

Chubasco: Formed from a low-pressure system off the Cuban city of Carpentier, these winds carry rains over Central America and other parts of the Caribbean and can last for one hundred years.

Descuernacabras: A wind strong enough to unhorn goats. This has been observed only once, in the province of Oriente.

Eurus: The unlucky wind that blows from the eastern coast of Cuba. Though at first it brings warm rains to the capital, these soon turn violent.

Huracán: The severe wind that periodically brings the Caribbean to its knees. The storm's violence is belied by a calm, quiet core that has fooled optimists down through the ages. The name derives from the god Huracán who, jealous of his brother's fine creations, decided he would dedicate his life to tearing down the beauty of this world. Huracán has a long beard, arms that flail in counterclockwise spirals, and in old times was often depicted smoking a cigar.

Foehn: A wind that begins innocently enough on the lee side of a mountain. Born warm, dry, and smaller than a grain of sand, it grows in both strength and heat as it travels down the slope, scorching everything in its path, including sugarcane. When it passes at night, its presence can still be detected in the morning by the faint sweet smell lingering in the air.

Notus: The south wind that beckons the huracán and sets the brightest star in the firmament, though it would deny both of these charges.

Zephyr: The gentlest of the Caribbean winds, the zephyr blows from the west, originating in the great cave of Santa Catalina in Matanzas. It smells of fruit and young grass and can turn the most violent jealousy into a field of hyacinth.

The Parachute Maker
BY OVID RODRIGUES

In the foothills of the mighty Sierra, facing the great bay of Cienfuegos, in the little village of Aquilo (now erased from the maps), there once lived a modest maker of parachutes. He was a lover of adjectives, and a bit long-winded, but otherwise lived simply and quietly in his thatched-roof hut.

The parachute maker, whose name was Belafonte, was born in Aquilo, as were his father and his grandfather before him. It was the same story on his mother's side, though maternal lineage is not usually recorded this way. In short, Belafonte's family had never known any other place but Aquilo.

For as long as anyone could remember, the village had been isolated from the rest of Cuba. Some people said this was because outsiders attributed a terrible temper and strange powers to the people of Aquilo. It may be true that others believed the calumny—Cubans are well known for their superstitions—but it was nevertheless nonsense, the typical kind of story that city people like to spin about country people. In fact, the people of Aquilo were just like other people. What was different was the weather. Aquilo sat at the particular convergence of several phenomena that were unexplained at the time but which we now understand as being primarily caused by a foehn, a wind capable of quickly raising temperatures by adiabatic compression (it is well known for its ability to induce bad moods as well as melt ice cream cones in two seconds flat). This wind, generated by the mountain slope directly behind Aquilo, contributed to cyclogenic conditions whose causes and effects would require several pages of graphs and equations to explain. For our purposes here, it suffices to say that Aquilo was always windy. In fact, wind was such a constant in Aquilo that there was no word for "windy," windiness being the normal condition. Similarly, there was no word for "calm" either, as the villagers had no experience of windless days. What the people of Aquilo did have was several variations—up to two hundred thirteen, by some counts—on the word "viento" that included designations for a caressing wind ("terciopielago"); a strong, temperate wind that came down the mountains in the early evening ("barbadeboreas"); a hot, steady wind ("horniento"); and a very, very hot foehn that changed direction at noon and blew up the mountain ("liber-notus").

Like many ancient peoples, the villagers of Aquilo worshipped the wind (whom they called Aquilo the Great), which provided them with electricity (every home naturally had a windmill) and a reliable constant in their lives. It should be no surprise to the student of evolutionary biology to learn that the Aquilinos had, over the years, adapted both physically and mentally to the reality of their windy village. The typical Aquilino face was flat across the cheekbones, with eyes narrowed into a permanent squint. The hair was always worn short. The people's mood—when not affected by the foehn—was particularly breezy and light. They farmed and tended goats. The women made popovers. And they did all this with uncommon swiftness. But it should be no surprise that for their main livelihood, the Aquilinos had chosen to make parachutes. It's not clear how the industry first arrived in Aquilo. Some said it had been developed by a native Aquilino, Esteban Bañes, who got the idea for building a parachute as he watched a plastic bag caught in the updraft of a strong horniento. Historians, who have never appreciated the value of a good anachronism, dispute this account, as well as many others in this story. They contend that parachutes had been brought to Aquilo by a stranger named Stefan Banic, who spoke a bizarre language. According to this version, Stefan remained in the village for a few years until he was finally made mad by the foehn and either vanished into the air or returned home. But Stefan (or Esteban) left behind his aerodynamic secrets, and by the time of the wars, the villagers were doing a brisk business in parachute making or, to use the more appropriate expression, envelope design. As the global economy developed and distant countries fought one another for dominance, more and more of the great powers found themselves outsourcing envelope production to Aquilo. So the village flourished, buoyed by the wings of history. Or something like that.

All would have been well, except that Aquilo, aside from the wind, was no different from any other village anywhere else in the world. It had its farmers and its merchants, its workers as well as its bosses. And not everyone was good. In those years, two things were indispensable to the craft of parachute making. One was silk; the other was the sewing machine. Now, the silk distributor was an honest and affable fellow named Mauricio. He bought his fabric wholesale in the capital, had it transported by mules to Aquilo, and sold it at a profit that was neither austere nor predatory. Like many honest men, Mauricio delighted in pleasing others. So he would often go out of his way to arrange for a particular color or a special weave. This especially endeared him to Belafonte, who was rapidly becoming known as Aquilo's master envelope maker. While all the villagers could turn out good parachutes, Belafonte's work was on another level: magnificent creations that today would be hanging in museums as works of art.

Unfortunately, Seraphim, the agent for the sewing machines, was neither honest nor beloved. He had managed to get an exclusive contract for the distribution of the machines, and he marked them up so high that they became unaffordable. As a consequence, Aquilinos were forced to lease the sewing machines on something called layaway, paying a few pesos each month to essentially rent the machines, which they knew they would never come to own. Then, as now, the world market for sewing machines was dominated by a single North American firm. Its English name could be mispronounced in Spanish in such a way as to render it unacceptably vulgar. So the product of this particular North American company was known as Cantante in Aquilo and, in spite of the beautiful creations it produced, its song was ultimately a sad one. Every few years, Belafonte would talk about traveling overseas himself and appealing to the makers of Cantante in person, but nothing came of these threats.

Overseas trips were expensive and stressful, and after a few days of storm and bluster, Belafonte would calm down and resume his work, which was one of the few things that brought him joy.

Rumors of the Aquilinos' discontent naturally reached Seraphim. But his riches put him beyond such cares. Alone among the villagers, Seraphim did not work as a parachute maker, the wealth from his distribution deal being so great as to nearly overwhelm him. He lived with his wife and three boys on a huge ranch up the hill, occupying the highest property in Aquilo. In the evenings, he would repair to his terrace with a good brandy and look out over the dim lights of Aquilo. He liked to sit there until it was dark, listening to the hum of all those Cantantes, which to him made the most pleasing music in all the world.

Seraphim amused himself by collecting horses; and by the time of our story, he had amassed an impressive stable that the villagers estimated at three thousand, though in reality the number was closer to seventy-five. Though he kept a few Tolfetanos and Swedish Ardennes, most of Seraphim's horses were Lipizzans—those mighty warhorses beloved down the ages. But his favorite horse, the one on which he lavished the most attention, was a rare white Thoroughbred stallion named Markab. Markab was a true white horse (unlike the Lipizzans, which, as anyone who has done an afternoon's research on this could tell you, are born dark and get progressively lighter as they age). Markab rose to almost eighteen hands high, and his eyes were the color of the twilight sky. On weekends, Seraphim would ride him down to the village, trotting a few laps around the square before taking Markab to El Rey's for ice cream. The horse seemed to favor pistachio—always served on a sugar cone—a preference that the sycophant owner of El Rey's enshrined in the menu by renaming a double scoop of pistachio El Markab. After their snack, man and horse would stand in the middle of the square to be admired. No one really remembers when the tradition started, but sometime in the years before the Great Crisis, one little boy had the courage to walk up to the horse and pat him. Others soon followed. Seraphim not only allowed this, but as time passed, he seemed to welcome it. Now and then he would direct a kind word to one of the children. A stranger seeing this—perhaps you—would regard Seraphim with a softened heart. You might begin to doubt what the Aquilinos said about him. Seraphim was becoming an old man, after all, and the kindness he showed the children was proof that in his powerful body there dwelled a gentle spirit. No. It is true that Seraphim was not all bad—who is?—but bear in mind that it is easy enough to be kind to children and cripples, especially when the evil of one's ways makes one eager to mitigate one's sins in the eyes of God and man. Believe me: the horse alone was blameless.

Though Seraphim doted on his Thoroughbred, he himself most closely resembled a Lipizzan. He had an unusually long head (even for an Aquilino), which sat atop a neck that arched back, giving him a bearing that accentuated his standoffish nature. His small ears were set high on his head and his flat Aquilino face (rather more convex in profile than normal) was dominated by his enormous brown eyes. When he was angry, which was often, his nostrils flared, revealing a tangle of white hair. He was powerfully built, from his wide chest to his muscular legs, which, in the summer, he was fond of showing off. This strong body, however, seemed to teeter on a pair of unusually small feet, an anatomical anomaly in Aquilo and one that invariably produced quiet snickers whenever he passed. In sum, Seraphim was not a good-looking man, and this shortcoming exacerbated his unpopularity, for as everyone knows, all sorts of sins are forgiven the beautiful.

Belafonte was such a creature. He was a bit above the average height of an Aquilino, and his light, thin limbs gave him the appearance of being even taller. One never saw him plodding along in Aquilo—no, Belafonte seemed to soar. To his many admirers, it seemed he was one and the same element with the wind that gamboled down those narrow streets of cobblestone. Though he was by then in his early thirties, Belafonte retained a delicate, boyish face and happy, curious eyes. It was a source of constant frustration to the mothers of the town that Belafonte had steadfastly refused marriage, preferring to spend solitary hours in his little thatched hut on the windiest bluff of Aquilo. He seemed to care for nothing else but making parachutes. And long after most of the Aquilinos had risen from their Cantantes and made their way to the village center for dinner and drinks, Belafonte remained at his machine. Often, when the villagers returned home from their late-night partying, they noticed that Belafonte's light was still on and his graceful silhouette bent over his current production. They were just parachutes, but Belafonte showered them with the disproportionate love of the obsessed. Like most artists, he gave his creations much more attention than they were worth. These were, after all, only parachutes destined for distant wars, not royal boudoirs. And yet, you wouldn't know it from examining the envelopes that Belafonte produced. It is really a shame that not one of those magnificent chutes survived: every one (except his final creation) burned on the fields of Europe. What a treasure the world lost—one of many it would never know. Belafonte took special care with even the standard-issue envelopes. Where others were content to stitch together the usual camouflage balloon as quickly as they could, Belafonte embellished even his ordinary works in subtle ways. Sometimes he would line the inside in iridescent silver, to give the falling airman the little bit of pleasure and private surprise that makes life worth living. Sometimes he would stitch sayings along the inner hem: *Live thy life as if it were spoil and pluck the joys that fly*. Belafonte stitched these by hand, in gold thread, on the inside, and there's no proof that the terrified airmen even saw them. If one of them chanced to look up, what did he imagine on reading *He rode upon a cherub, and did fly: yea, he did fly upon the wings of wind*? And still, with no hope of readers for his work, Belafonte wrote. There's no explanation for this impulse other than his innate playfulness, the inner joy that blows through certain people and rearranges notions, sweeps away cobwebs, transforms rigid ideas into odd and pliable shapes.

In fact, Belafonte had for some time been experimenting with alternative shapes. Of course, orders had to be filled, and the requisitions were exact: so many inches, so much weight distribution. Belafonte never forgot that his creations were, above everything, utilitarian things. He never went in for the dissident talk during the height of the European war, that proposed that Aquilo was indirectly increasing suffering around the world by supplying the war machine. Some of the younger men and women had called for a strike, suggesting that Aquilo's expertise would be better directed at building touring balloons for the forthcoming Chicago World's Fair. Belafonte would have none of that. The Aquilino envelopes were not just beautiful; they were lifesaving creations capable of buoying a man to safety. These were the big themes: fear and redemption. How could that compare to the antics of silly tourists in a hot air balloon? Belafonte would become even more animated than usual when talking of the soldiers his work was saving. What a feeling it must have been, he told me once in his shop, for those men—who moments before had been jolted out of their fiery machines—to find themselves floating silently, slowly, to earth. But the strikers got their way, at least for a while. And for about two months, parachute production almost came to a halt in Aquilo. Belafonte did his best to increase his pace, working sometimes through the night to fill the orders that were piling up. Understandably, he did not produce his best work during this time. But Aquilo met its targets and the contracts were saved—at least that time. When everyone returned to work, Belafonte returned to his art. Alternative shapes. Yes, for a while, as I said, Belafonte had been experimenting with alternative shapes. Though the others said that only bell shapes would fly, Belafonte proved that, with careful calculation, the wind could be distributed over an amazingly diverse number of surfaces. His first one was a balloon shaped like a giant apple, done up in shiny candy-red silk that Mauricio had brought in from the capital specially for him. No one in Aquilo will forget the day that Belafonte tested it, drifting down from a spot just above Seraphim's ranch on a beautiful terciopielago that was blowing that day. By the time Belafonte floated over the square, most of the village had come out to watch. The children cheered. Beneath the giant apple, Belafonte seemed no bigger than its seed, a wisp of a man, hands outstretched as he faced the sea. Next came an almost exact replica of his cottage, complete with thatched roof: a cylindrical envelope that Belafonte had decorated with red and yellow flowers. This one he tested at dawn, when an horniento blew strong enough to propel even a real cottage over the foothills. Those villagers who were awake reported the flight as a sort of hallucination, as if Belafonte's cottage had somehow come loose from its moorings to haunt their dreams.

The parachute maker managed these creations on his days off, for he continued to produce regulation canopies for the war effort, his Cantante singing regularly into the early morning hours. Now and then, he included one of his alternative forms in his shipment, expertly folding and packing it with the others. He liked to imagine the surprise of those soldiers who, having ejected from a burning plane or leaped out the chute door, machine gun in hand, found themselves suddenly floating to earth beneath a gold silken sun or a giant banana that rustled in the wind. Belafonte had hit a certain rhythm in his work and was happy.

But this story whirls and twirls in concentric circles, doesn't it? And one day came the Great Crisis, though it's important to note that "Great Crisis" is the name the villagers gave it afterward. At the beginning, no one could really know that anything like a Great Crisis was under way. Maybe a mini crisis, or a downturn, something that would blow over soon—that's what everyone said when the first orders of the month came in ten chutes short of the previous month. Some of the parachute makers didn't even notice, or if they did, they said it was due to the normal cycles of commerce and was nothing to worry about. The Aquilinos, understand, were more immune than most people to the battering winds of fate. They had just learned to take whatever came, adjust their paths through the valleys, turn their backs on the worst of it, and carry on. So they did.

The following month, the orders came in fifty short of the peak. But still there were some in the village who argued that pessimistic predictions were so much bluster. This went on for a few months, the orders falling or sometimes briefly rallying only to plunge even more. Then, as if matters weren't already bad enough, the war ended.

Reports began seeping into Aquilo of a worldwide downturn in the business cycle. The chute orders trickled away to nothing. The silk bolts piled up in Mauricio's storerooms. The nights of dinner and drinks grew fewer and fewer until the pub owners appealed to the villagers to return to their old ways. But though the villagers would have liked to, they could not. The little money that was left was needed for essentials. Restaurants and bars began to close. Where once the villagers had dined on caviar and imported cheeses, now they turned to the fruits of their own land, surviving on the old staples: black beans and bramble berries. A year into the crisis, when conditions were at their worst, a consortium of women hit on the idea of sewing backpacks and purses out of the stockpiled fabric. Soon Aquilo, the proud village that had turned out so many soaring monuments to freedom and possibility, was stitching together lightweight bags decorated with kittens and smiley faces. It was humiliating work, but it kept the village aloft for a while. Even Belafonte contributed to the efforts, turning out bright little purses on his Cantante. But he never abandoned his balloons. During those long dark months, he hung on to the lightness of his character by working on what was to be his last creation. He worked in secret, from a private pattern. But word got out about the absurd lengths of silk that he was buying from Mauricio. Some said Belafonte was building the world's greatest balloon. Others thought he was being kind to Mauricio, simply relieving his old friend of excess inventory.

For half a year, Belafonte and the villagers were able to just break even with the income from their purses. But distribution was slow, and the market for their product as depressed as they were. Before long the people of Aquilo were forced to accept their new poverty. The nation may have been talking of a general recovery, but it was clear that, in Aquilo at least, the jobs were not returning. The villagers had scrimped and saved everywhere they could. There was only one last expense to cut: the monthly payments for their sewing machines. This was not, as Seraphim claimed later, an organized move. There were no underground meetings where such an action was proposed. In fact, the first few villagers who began to renege on their payments did so in secret shame and alone. The Aquilinos were, for the most part, upright people, and they believed in fulfilling their obligations, even if said obligations were to a manipulative predator like Seraphim. At first, all continued as before. The renegers kept quiet and so did Seraphim. One month passed, two, then three. Little by little, more villagers stopped making their payments—though at the time this was a fact known only to Seraphim. One Sunday, Seraphim failed to appear in the square with Markab. Those villagers who had not been keeping up with their Cantante payments grew nervous. Each was privately afraid of being exposed in public by Seraphim. Meanwhile, the other villagers, who had not yet stopped making payments but were thinking of doing so, began to hope to themselves that something had happened to Seraphim, something permanent that would allow them to do so. "What could be the matter with the old man?" they said to one another. Chattering and speculation continued as the sun sank lower in the sky and still Seraphim had not appeared atop his white horse.

"Someone should go and check on him," said one man.

"Nonsense," said the man's wife.

"Whatever could be the matter?"

At this, Belafonte at last stepped forward. "Friends," he said. "I have a shameful confession to make. Three months ago, being low on funds and behind in my work as well as very hungry, I stopped making payments on my Cantante. Perhaps because of this, Seraphim has decided to snub all of us."

The children in the audience began to cry. But to Belafonte's surprise, no general gasp followed his confession. Another man stepped forward.

"You are not alone, Belafonte," he said. "I too stopped making payments on my Cantante last month."

Suddenly, it was like a great tide loosed. Men and women stepped forward, many of them now laughing and clapping their hands.

"We too stopped making payments!"

With that, those few holdouts who had continued to make the crushing payments to Seraphim decided then and there to put a stop on their checks and not give that snake another dime. The square erupted into celebration and, anticipating their newfound savings, the villagers stormed the pubs, making the beleaguered owners quite happy.

Now, as you may have guessed, Seraphim was watching all this through a pair of high-powered binoculars from his mountain ranch.

"Aha," he said.

The following morning, though it was a workday, Seraphim appeared in the square atop a freshly washed and bejeweled Markab. The sight of them actually caused an audible gasp among the few villagers who had gathered under the arcades for brunch. Seraphim sat high and mighty on his horse. He wore rings on his pinkies and a black hat on his white hair. His black suit was freshly pressed. And Markab—Markab looked like a dream. The villagers guessed that the old man had spent the night brushing and currying him, for Markab's coat, always beautiful, shone as never before, and within the braids of his mane were interwoven hundreds of diamonds that glittered like stars in a white heaven.

Seraphim pulled Markab along the square before coming to rest in the center as before. He was waiting for word to spread, which it did. Within a quarter of an hour, the square was filled, though most villagers wore large floppy hats to hide their faces and stood back under the shadows so as not to be recognized. Still, as you can see, curiosity is stronger than shame, because they came.

"Neighbors," began Seraphim, "we have lived together in peace and harmony since the time of the first wind. We have prospered together, we have dined together, we have grown wealthy together."

At this last mention, a ripple of snickers went through the crowd, but Seraphim ignored them. He held one hand to his hat. A terciopielago was blowing through the square. While Seraphim spoke, Markab stared straight ahead, as if he'd heard this all before.

"I have always strived to provide the best services to the people of Aquilo, the highest-quality products. As you know, these do not come cheap. There are today available certain sewing machines manufactured in China that would be far less expensive to import. But I have resisted. I have provided to you only the finest equipment from North America, built by people for whom high quality and honesty are national characteristics."

Another snicker went up among the crowd. Markab fluttered his long eyelashes, but Seraphim did not skip a beat.

"Now we are in the grips of a Great Crisis. A few of you—not a great many, but a significant few—have decided to take matters into your own hands and stop payment on your Cantantes. While I can understand the impulse, I would like to remind you that this action is completely dishonest and goes against all our values as Aquilinos."

Here Seraphim paused, pulling the reins on Markab until man and horse began a small trot in place. The villagers retreated farther into the shadows.

The wind picked up. Seraphim removed his hat. "I will give those of you who are scofflaws two weeks to return to your payments and, in the interest of community harmony, will forgive the last month of debt."

The villagers debated this last point for hours after Seraphim had dug his spurs into Markab's flanks and retreated to his ranch.

"Forgive the last month of debt," said a man named Juan.

"Why, the old serpent is desperate," said another man, also named Juan.

Belafonte wasn't so sure, but he remained quiet as the others debated what to do. They had embarked on their defiance separately, in private, but were now bound to their decisions as one. With his speech, Seraphim had marked the camps and the Aquilinos had the first inkling of their superior numbers. By the end of the afternoon, the men and women (for women had equal decision-making powers in Aquilo) had decided to continue their defiance.

"With what I've paid over the years, I could have bought my own factory of Cantantes," said a woman named Maria.

"He has been bleeding us dry," said her sister. "Why did we ever agree to such terms?" She added, "The fault is ours," by which she meant the ones among them who had urged the rest to accept the terms. Everyone knew who they were. There's no need to further embarrass them here.

Belafonte returned to his thatched hut without saying a word and went right back to work. He worked more furiously than ever, rarely venturing out to talk to the villagers. Some said he had become rather stuck-up from all the praise for his alternative shapes. Others said he was just shy. But most people didn't think of Belafonte at all, preferring to concentrate on their own problems, which were numerous.

The months wore on. By the end of the year, the only person still making payments on her Cantante was old Maria, who was Seraphim's mother. So the day came for Seraphim to make another appearance atop Markab in the square. This time, Markab's mane was woven with rubies as well as diamonds and Seraphim wore a giant emerald on his pinkie, as if to say, "I'm so rich that I don't need your money—it's only a matter of principle."

And that's exactly what he said: "My fellow Aquilinos, I am so rich that I don't need your money. However, the payments have become a matter of principle."

He warned them that he had been in touch with the factory in North America and the owners were not happy. They had just come through a strike in a place called Clydeside that most people, including the villagers, had never heard of.

"The North Americans are not pleased with the turn of events here in Aquilo," Seraphim said. "I have assured them that our people are honest and good for their word. I have done my best to ensure that they do not meddle with our affairs here. But . . ."

"But what?" shouted Juan.

Seraphim turned to him. "But I cannot stop them from taking matters into their own hands."

"Is that so?" Juan said. "Why should we be beholden to a craven foreign company?" He stepped forward from the shadows and jutted his chin at the horse. Markab blinked slowly. Juan turned to the villagers. "My people, it so happens that I have a cousin in Spain. The sewing machines are sold there also and are heavily advertised." He reached into his coat pocket and produced a card that, naturally, flapped thunderously in the wind. "And she sent me this!"

Those villagers nearest Juan pressed close. There was a loud gasp that rippled through the courtyard as the placard made its way around. When it came to Belafonte, he read slowly out loud:

It has been said that every native Spanish woman is energetic; whether she be from Andalusia or Asturias, the south or the north, she has none of the Creole languor of the Spanish-descended woman of Cuba, Mexico, and tropical America.

"Creole languor!" gasped Maria. "Why, this is outrageous. We don't even make that dish."

"There's more," shouted Juan. "Read the rest, Belafonte."

There is vim and force in the native Spaniard, and she is usually a better type than the man of her race. Our artist has sent to us five photos, showing distinct types of Spanish women: the Basque from the Pyrenees, the industrious Catalonian, a blue-eyed blonde from Salamanca, a stout Andalusian of the provincial class, a patriotic Galician from Corunna, and the one whom we present from Old Seville with her lover. How characteristic are the accessories! The woman is industrious, and regards with an air of distinct disapproval the weak-faced individual before her with his guitar and glass of wine.

"What's wrong with a glass of wine?" shouted Juan, the pub owner.

Belafonte shook his head but continued to read. Markab began to prance in place.

> Many a Spanish woman would now be driven to hard
> straits were it not for the Singer sewing machine, which
> is furnished to her on the most liberal terms of payment;
> thus, she easily becomes self-supporting.

"So it's the men who are lazy!" shouted Juan.

"And in English to top it all off!" shouted Maria. "Why those no-good ... Singerados!"

"Forget it, Seraphim. Tell your masters that we won't pay another dime," shouted her sister.

Through all this, Seraphim had remained quiet on his horse. Perhaps he had reached a decision. He said no more, dug his spurs into Markab, and was gone.

The advertising placard was returned to the original Juan. Many of the villagers remained in the square. And as soon as the sun went down, they went into the pubs to each order a single glass of wine.

The mass defiance seemed to reinvigorate Aquilo. The people still had the same problems—in particular, no money—but now they were all involved in something together. They were collectively telling the rich guy to shove off. And it made them happy. In the mornings, the villagers went singing to their machines; in the afternoons, they gathered in the square to plot, or just drink, and wait for Seraphim's next appearance. They had to wait almost three months. During this time, Belafonte was working almost twenty hours a day. When he appeared in public, the villagers scarcely recognized him; he'd become so gaunt and gray, and his fingers were covered with scabs.

Seraphim reappeared in the square on an especially windy day. The season of the liber-notus had come early, and all the men were forced to leave their hats at home that afternoon. They stood bareheaded before Seraphim and Markab, who was now adorned with pearls as well as the aforementioned rubies and diamonds.

Seraphim waited a long time before speaking. When he finally began, it was with a long and pointless prologue about his father and his father's father before him. He talked about the founding of Aquilo—all of it myth, since no one could possibly remember that far back—and how when ill winds began to blow the tradition had always been to snuff them out quickly. Never mind what to modern ears sounds like mixing metaphors; this is how Seraphim talked, and there's nothing we can do about it. The more he talked, the more his voice rose. The villagers, sensing an interesting confrontation, streamed into town. Soon all of Aquilo was in the square, just as Seraphim wanted. This time, no child ventured to touch Markab—the children did not even have to be scolded by their mothers. The little ones sensed that something big had changed in Aquilo forever.

Seraphim paused and took a sip of water from a plastic bottle hanging on his belt. "People of Aquilo," he said, almost shouting now. "Your actions have saddened me deeply. I who have always had your best interests in mind. I who struggled to bring the latest technology so you might be liberated from the old ways. How long, ladies and gentlemen, would it take you to stitch a chute by hand, the way your great-grandmothers and great-grandfathers before you were forced to do? And what is the thanks I get for helping to increase your productivity fourfold, for invigorating the industry, for making Aquilo a world center of parachute making? What do I get? Answer me!"

Some of the villagers, it must be admitted, felt a twinge of shame. They could have asked for a renegotiation of the terms. They might have tried to reason with Seraphim instead of abruptly tearing up their contracts. Perhaps this all might have been handled differently.

But their softened hearts were soon to harden, because what happened next was without precedent in all the districts of that mountain town. The liber-notus was blowing hard now, and this may have accounted for the anxiety and panic that began to spread in the square. Even Markab seemed to catch the feeling, taking little mincing steps in place as if his legs hurt him. Seraphim's voice had become shrill.

At first, the men streaming down from the hills seemed like a vision. The villagers stared silently, each afraid of speaking and being discovered mad. But then they turned to one another and pointed at the sight before them: an army of men, very tall and fair, walking down the hills with ease, each of them pushing a wheelbarrow full of . . . full of something dark. Seraphim continued to speak as if nothing had happened, not even turning to see what it was people were pointing at. He already knew, of course.

Juan was the first to understand. "Our machines!" he shouted. "They've confiscated our machines!" There was a roar of incomprehension and the Aquilinos made a move to rush the wheelbarrow men. Suddenly, from the streets feeding into the square, there appeared an army of men riding Seraphim's warhorses. The men wore guards on their legs and carried Louisville sluggers, the old ones, made of white ash. The villagers retreated. The wheelbarrow men kept coming down from the hills, carrying Aquilo's Cantantes.

Seraphim allowed a smile to cross his face. He raised his hands.

"People of Aquilo."

The crowd quieted.

"You have left me with no other choice but to reclaim what is mine." He held up his hands again to stop the rumbling. "Yes, what is mine. I hold here the contract that each and every one of you signed. I know it by memory. Shall I recite? 'I hereby acknowledge that said machine shall remain the sole property of Seraphim Blas for the life of the product. I understand I am only the lessee, and right of possession may be revoked at any time due to nonpayment or whatever other whim comes over the owner.'"

Seraphim waved the paper. "Did you hear that? Did you think I would not move to enforce this document? What kind of society are we living in if basic contracts are not honored? What society would we become if people no longer kept true to their word, no longer respected the law? I have never claimed any right to your artistic product—only to the means of production. And each and every one of you took advantage of that. Had I insisted on a percentage of your sales, what a wealthy man I would be!"

By this time the wheelbarrow men had gathered in the square. The women began to sob. "Friends," Seraphim said. "I will ignore your hissing. I am giving each of you one last chance to keep your machines. I will call out your names, one by one. Approach with the money that is owed and your machine will be returned to you. . . ."

It was the saddest day in Aquilo. By the time the sun rose over the valley the next morning, every single Cantante lay smashed to pieces on the square. The villagers had been too stunned (and scared) to resist, and the entire tragedy had taken on the aspect of a ritual. Seraphim would call the villager's name; the Aquilino would step forward and plead his case. Some promised to have the money tomorrow. Some cursed Seraphim openly. But each time, the drama ended the same way: a machine would be taken from the wheelbarrow, the villager would begin to sob, and then the Louisville Sluggers would come down. It took all that day and night to destroy the machines.

Belafonte did not wait for it to be over. As soon as he saw the men with the wheelbarrows, he had sprinted to his thatched hut, squinting his eyes against the fierce wind. His machine was gone, of course, but his envelopes had been left untouched. That was all he wanted to know. What man, toiling at work for another man, has not dreamed of flight? Our hero was modest, but he'd been tied to the ground in a place of wind and stars. He was hardly the first in the history of Cuba or the world to look to the skies for freedom. Think of Matías, the Little Prince, Bellerophon.

Belafonte's last envelope was now complete. He knew that Seraphim would not long endure defiance. So he had worked until his eyes closed on their own, awaking slumped over his Cantante to start again on his greatest creation. The night of the smashed Cantantes, Belafonte had been the only Aquilino who enjoyed a deep and restful sleep.

The next morning, those villagers still in the square watched Belafonte ascend the mountain, carrying a large golden backpack and a pair of reins made of silk thread. Some of them called out to Belafonte, but he was too far away, with the liber-notus already at his back. He did not turn around until he had reached Seraphim's ranch, by which time the wind was so hot that it had begun to bake the wild rosemary, filling the valley with sweet astringency.

~

Last year, researching an article on Belafonte, I came upon a Web site dedicated to the British Airborne, where I clicked on a link that brought me to a page that included another link that brought me to another page, and so on until, in one of those epic pixelated meanderings that we undertake now in lieu of the great journeys of old, I alighted on a Google Books page. And there I found a strange poem by William Wordsworth about a boy who flies to heaven on a boat to examine the stars. It began, to my surprise, with a tribute to Belafonte, the modest maker of parachutes:

> *There's something in a flying horse,*
> *There's something in a huge balloon . . .*

From: The Poets

To: Herberto Quain

Date: May 23, 1923

Re: Your book

Dear Mr. Quain:

It has come to our attention that you intend to publish an anthology of our work. While we are flattered to be remembered (so many of us worked in obscurity for so long), we must nevertheless ask you to abandon your project.

Because we are such a diverse group of writers, you may imagine that the reasons for asking you to cease and desist are equally numerous. Many among us object, first, to being lumped into that most discredited of categories: *Cuban*. Do you intend our work to languish in the special-interest section of the great library? Are you actively working to keep us tied to a single identity? Frankly, we are mystified. As you no doubt understand by now, much of our lifework was and continues to be dedicated to the idea of escaping the bonds imposed by others. And now you come, an outsider, to impose on us a doomed structure. It is quite unacceptable.

Which brings us to another objection: Who are you? You are neither Cuban nor a poet yourself.

And (if we are to be frank) you are not even real. This Roscommon that you purport to be from is imaginary, a dream dreamed by someone else, an unknown person who has imbued you with memories and facts which are neither. We are sorry to have to speak hard truths of which even you may not be aware. But many of us object to your taking upon yourself a project for which you are not qualified.

Furthermore, as we understand it, you have not moved to obtain copyrights for our work, which as you know the government has granted all artists to the end of time in perpetuity. Publishing these works will be a breach of law as it is currently understood and will be prosecuted. There is, as you may be aware, at least one attorney among us.

Finally, we object to the narrow scope of your vision as reflected in your working title, "History of the Cuban Poets According to Quain." As one of us said, Quain, quién? What gives you the authority? To be done properly, this collection should be put together by a genuine scholar, preferably Cuban himself, and not an Irishman who faked his qualifications to work for our National Library. For these and many other reasons, we respectfully ask that you leave the Cubans to the Cubans. We want no part in this book. If you have further questions, you may contact Jane Smith, who is representing us in this matter. She may be reached at

555-962-4661 between nine A.M. and five P.M. Eastern Standard or by e-mail at jsmiththecuban@gmail.com.

Sincerely,

Johnny Aldo, Laika Almeida, Alex Carpenter, C. Casey, Celestino d'Alba, Teresa de la Landre, Rosaura del Bosque, Ernesto del Camino, Vietor Fúka, Carla Gades, Silas Haslam, Ana Menéndez, Zanem Neenda, Victoria O'Campo, Ovid Rodrigues, Jane Smith, et al.

From: Herberto Quain

To: The Poets

Date: August 9, 1912

Re: Re: Your book

Dear respected poets:

My apologies for taking so long to respond—time is not what it used to be. I promise to consider your request, or at the very least, to make the reader aware of it.

But I'm afraid that I must state, for the record, several objections to your objections. It is you who have not understood your own work. This is forgivable, given the constraints of your narrow lives. Each of you writes in isolation, without seeing the structure that you are nevertheless building. You need me to give you meaning, but you are too full of individual self-importance (your "joint" letter notwithstanding) to understand this.

Furthermore, it is you who are invented, not I. I enjoyed a long and independent life for decades before you appeared in this universe. I therefore object to the quite disrespectful tone of your letter.

As for your laughable objection to my not being Cuban, why should that matter? Can only Cubans understand Cubans? Or are Cubans the only ones in this world looking for a hidden passage, a way out of our maze? You object to being tethered to a single identity and yet you retreat into it for protection. You contradict yourselves, which is no surprise: such is the lot of your countrymen and of your chosen professions.

As for copyrights, I am willing to take my chances. Many of you are already dead, or soon will be and thus will be on the other side of the conventions you now cling to. I am willing, however, to make a small concession on the title, and you'll be pleased to learn that I have already changed it.

In closing, I would like to address myself to the one mathematician among you. You know who you are. Perhaps you alone can understand the scope of my project, which began with a simple equation:

$$z \begin{vmatrix} y_1 \begin{vmatrix} & x_1 \\ & x_2 \\ & \end{vmatrix} \\ y_2 \begin{vmatrix} & \bar{x}_3 \\ & x_4 \end{vmatrix} \end{vmatrix}^{7}$$

But I have modified it slightly as my scholarship demanded:

---

7. "Examination of the Works of Herbert Quain," http://frot.org/borges/quain.html.

$$(x+a)^n = \sum_{k=0}^{n}\binom{n}{k}x^k a^{n-k}$$

Or, more simply put:

$$x_n = x_{n-1} + x_{n-2}$$

Never forget the one law of the universe, which is that everything is like everything else even if it happens only once, to us, which is to say: to me.

Equally sincerely,

Herberto Quain

Redstone
BY C. CASEY

My grandfather was born on December 17, 1903, which was also the day, as he often reminded us, that the Wright brothers made their historic flight. He was five years old when he discovered this coincidence, and ever after would say he had been born to the sky. He claimed later that as a boy he had been fascinated by flying things—birds, balloons, kites. This precocious awareness of his was, of course, impossible for the grandchildren to verify except through a few, perhaps apocryphal, stories. For though my grandfather wasn't, by the current customs of provenance, Cuban, he did seem to have acquired something of the island propensity for tall tales.

Certainly there had been little in his background to suggest a career in aeronautics. He'd been born in Havana to American parents. His father, a newspaperman, had been stationed in Cuba during the war. And though my grandfather's mother frequently complained of the heat and insects (she was from an old Boston family), the three of them seem to have settled into the rhythm of the country well enough. In those years, people were still talking of the Portuguese awning maker who had made off in a balloon and had never been heard from again. This, too, seized the imagination of my grandfather, who, one spring morning in 1910, grabbed his father's black umbrella and launched himself from the third-floor balcony. He broke his right leg and three bones in his left foot, fractures which gave him trouble until the day he died. But his fascination with flight remained intact.

The family returned to the United States when my grandfather was eleven years old. His father and then his mother died soon after and he was sent to live with cousins of his father's in Huntsville, Alabama. (Yes, this is the same Huntsville, Alabama, where in 2010, a disgruntled scientist murdered three colleagues at a faculty meeting—suggesting that perhaps something of the malignancy of violent creation can linger over a town for years, like a permanent smog.) This move no doubt scandalized the Boston side of the family, but as my grandfather told it, he was glad to be in the South, where both the weather and the food reminded him of his childhood in Cuba.

In 1917, claiming he was eighteen, he joined the army and served a year in Europe. When he returned, he married his childhood sweetheart and enrolled in college right there in Huntsville, where ten years later he received his PhD. There's no evidence that my grandfather suffered any trauma from that most bloody war. Grandmother always said that he returned almost the same man he had left and slept like a baby for the rest of his life. He rarely talked about the war with us grandchildren, or at least with the girls. After he died, one of my male cousins told me that Grandfather had confessed to him that he had once killed a German soldier with his own hands to escape captivity. The details, so far as my cousin remembered them, were hazy. Were they hazy from Grandfather's memory and his lying, or from my cousin's memory and his lying? Impossible to tell. But the story, at least in my cousin's inexpert hands, did not have the kind of drama that would lend it to retelling and so it was soon forgotten and never spoken of again. One thing that did seem certain, even to me, the youngest, was that Grandfather did not have any objections to war. You'd think that someone who had lived through the Great War would have become a pacifist (as so many did), or at least would have shunned military work. On the contrary, my grandfather embraced it, though we didn't suspect the extent of his involvement until many years later.

Grandfather was eighty-six years old when the Berlin Wall fell, and I was glad he was alive to see it. He had become frail in recent months, but the proclaimed end of the Cold War seemed to reinvigorate him. He would spend long hours in front of the television or on his shortwave, listening to reports, even in languages he could not understand, simply for the pleasure of hearing the excitement in the voices. I had just finished university and returned home that fall to look for a job—by this time we all lived in Miami, where my grandfather had moved after his retirement. I was able, then, to spend long afternoons with him, watching the footage and listening to his stories. He especially liked the stories of escape. He had a photographic memory, and as the television networks rolled black-and-white footage of attempts to get over the wall, he would anticipate the details and, often, the names. He remembered the name of the first person killed trying to escape over the wall: Günter Litwin. ("Assassinated August 24, 1961; you weren't even born yet.") But, not surprisingly, his memory was clearest for those escapes that had ended happily. One afternoon, when an old film began, Grandfather sat up in his chair and said, "1965. Stanislaus Gefreefer," pronouncing the name as if it had been on his tongue his whole life. We watched in silence as the footage showed a man propping a ladder against the wall, leaping over it, and falling into the back of a waiting truck on the other side. "Look at that happiness," my grandfather said. And there were tears in his eyes. Grandfather then began to recount more escapes, as if that image had loosened others in his mind. He told me of tunnels that young people built beneath the wall, tunnels that soon became escape passageways for children, parents, and even the frail and infirm like himself. One tunnel, he told me, was dug in a graveyard. "Families would come with carnations and peonies to lay on the graves," my grandfather said. "And they would kneel before the tombstones and sob and sob. And after they had sobbed away all their crocodile tears, they would simply vanish. As if swallowed by the earth, which of course, they had been." Then he smiled. "Who said the dead aren't useful?"

All this while, my grandfather was saving his favorite story, which he finally told me a few days later: the story of a family who flew over the wall in a hot air balloon. This story was most certainly false, I thought, a conflation of my grandfather's childhood memories of Cuba and his lifelong fascination with flying machines. As the television flickered with jubilant images, he told me of two families who concocted a bold, elaborate plan for escape after watching a child's balloon float innocently over the wall from the other side. Within days, the members of the families were slowly and secretly buying up small scraps of nylon. After almost a year, they had enough to stitch together to form an envelope (which Grandfather stressed is the correct term for the lightweight globe that most people call a "balloon"). During this time, my grandfather said, the women had also been secretly saving small amounts of their cooking fuel. The men fashioned a burner, and a basket. And one day, the families powered up the whole machine at the border. "And they just floated over the wall," Grandfather said. "What sublime beauty, what light and soundless joy they must have felt!" (Some years later, I was telling a friend this story and she said, "Oh, yeah, the Wetzels and Strlzycks. Disney made a movie about them." And so she robbed me of a little magic. But so it goes.)

We sat together like this many evenings, Grandfather recounting bits and pieces of his life, weaving them into the world's, as if his memory and history had fused and were now bubbling up, seeking new expression. The stories did not necessarily have a continuous narrative—they seemed, especially at the beginning, more like fragments of larger stories, ideas, and images snatched out of an undifferentiated well of experience. But slowly, they took shape. And some revealed themselves to me only many, many years later.

A little more than a month before he died, Grandfather walked into the library where I was working. He carried a stack of files, and when I saw him struggling under the weight, I leaped up to help him. He thanked me as I laid them on the table and pulled a chair for him. It took him a few moments to catch his breath.

"What is this," I joked, to fill in the time, "property deeds to the lavish mansions I'm going to inherit?"

"What?" he said. He was half deaf by then.

"Nothing," I said.

He nodded. "I had planned to give these to Charlie or Manny," he said, naming my two eldest cousins. "But you're the only one here at the moment, so you're stuck with it."

Over the next two hours, Grandfather told me a most extraordinary story. Most of it is declassified now, so I'm not risking anything by sharing the general outlines.

After World War II, the United States, fearing it was falling behind in weapons design, began to recruit German scientists in an effort called Operation Paperclip. Problem was that the mandate signed by Truman expressly forbade recruiting anyone who had been a member of the Nazi Party. Well, this was ridiculous, since to be a high-ranking scientist in Hitler's Germany, one had to be a member of the Nazi Party. The best rocket scientists, Wernher von Braun and Arthur Rudolph, had already been identified as a "menace." What to do? To get around Truman's order, the JIOA hatched a plan to imagine new pasts for the guys they wanted to bring over. Scrubbed clean, the German scientists were reborn in the United States as faultless as day-old babes. So purified, they earned security clearance and were moved to White Sands to begin working for Uncle Sam. "What a lucky break those guys caught," my grandfather said over and over again, more in awe than disgust. "Education, my dear, education will always save your skin. Don't let anyone tell you otherwise."

The focus of this first collaboration between the old Nazis and the fresh-faced Americans was the V-2 rocket. "You never heard of the V-2? Girls. The V-2 was supposedly the granddaddy of the German artillery force, though why this should be is beyond me. The rocket holds the distinction of having killed more people in its production than in its deployment," my grandfather said. "Me, I think the fascination with the V-2 had more to do with keeping it out of the Reds' hands than it did with the rocket's intrinsic qualities." I later learned, through Wikipedia, that some twenty thousand inmates at the infamous Mittelbau-Dora plant died during the production of the V-2s. "Of these, nine thousand died from exhaustion and collapse, three hundred fifty were hanged (including two hundred executed for acts of sabotage), and the remainder either were shot or died from disease or starvation." But whatever the reason, the U.S. military scrambled to get as many V-2 parts as it could. "I was in Las Cruces when the railcars started coming in," Grandfather told me. "Engines, tanks, gyroscopes, all the guts of these babies."

Here I stopped him. We knew he was an engineer and it was no secret that he had worked for the military. But we had never really explored the extent of his involvement. It turned out that Grandfather had been recruited into the weapons development laboratory in Huntsville while he was still a doctoral student there and had worked on top-secret projects in one way or another until his retirement. I have to admit that I swelled a little with pride to learn that Grandfather had been so wise and trusted in his time.

After recounting this brief history of his employment, Grandfather began to give me all sorts of technical information on the German rocket, pulling out papers and charts that, as far as I was concerned, could have been the blueprints for a quaint country chalet. Perhaps sensing my boredom, he cleared his throat. "Right. Well, I get a little carried away. But I want you to keep these. Maybe you aren't interested now, but maybe you will be someday. Or maybe your son will be." I don't think he believed any of this. I sense that the fall of the Berlin Wall and the flood of memories and stories had just made him eager to keep sharing more. Or perhaps, as my cousins later said, he simply wanted to unburden himself—to lighten the load, so to speak, for his final flight of no return.

As it turns out, the V-2 was important to my grandfather, not as a rocket, but because it was the precursor to the Redstone missile. The military launched the first Redstone in 1953. "It was the first missile in live nuclear tests," my grandfather said. And his voice was full of pride. It was, he said, the most important project he worked on during all his years.

It is no exaggeration to say that my grandfather knew the Redstone more intimately than he knew his own young children. He knew the blast yield and fuel capacity by memory. And all those years later, he could still remember the Redstone's length: 21.1 meters.

I did not dare ask him if he felt any guilt about his involvement. Not because I thought it would anger or—God forbid—sadden him, but because I feared it would reduce me in his eyes, reveal me to be a naive, soft fool. The only thing that seems to have depressed my grandfather in the years of his youth was the Soviet launching of Sputnik. "We had the superior scientists, materials, we had the work ethic, we had the benefits of freedom, and the Reds still beat us to space," my grandfather said. "That first week you could have heard a pin drop in the lab. Something had to be done." He turned to me. "So I suggested the Redstone. That part was my idea." He shook his head. "Though the venue was someone else's, someone in Washington. What did I know about train stations?"

By this time I was thoroughly confused. But that happened more and more in conversation with Grandfather, and I didn't think it proper to interrupt him. Besides, he wouldn't have heard me. "Twenty-one point one meters," my grandfather said. "That's about sixty-nine point three feet." He began to laugh, and that led to a coughing fit, and when the coughing was over, he wiped his tears. "We all should have known it wouldn't fit. But someone got it in his head to haul a Redstone over to New York and put it on display at Grand Central Station. Had to cut the ceiling to set it in place, that son-of-a-gun missile. What a beauty!"

With this last detail, I began to doubt my grandfather's story. I didn't doubt he had worked on the Redstone, though perhaps not to the extent that he hinted at. And maybe he did suggest some sort of publicity stunt. But I could not accept that the government would really think the American public would be impressed by the sight of a giant missile in New York City. What would be the point? And even if I could be persuaded to believe that such things made sense in those times, there was no way anyone would have suggested cutting into a ceiling to make it happen.

"What stories you have, Grandfather," I said.

"What?" he said.

~

I could find no work that fall or the following spring, so the next year, I returned to the university, to get my PhD. Something of what my grandfather had said to me that afternoon must have resonated and I opted for a career in the academy. Education, my dear, education will always save your skin.

In late 2000, I found myself in New York City for a conference. I'm embarrassed to admit that, at age thirty-three, I had never been to Manhattan. A colleague mentioned that I should not miss the newly renovated Grand Central Station. By that time, I had forgotten Grandfather's story, but I had a free afternoon and it was snowing and I could think of nothing better to do. I arrived just as a tour was beginning and joined it. It was led by a trim, energetic man. He carried a laser pointer and now and then directed it at particular aspects of the architecture that he wanted to talk about. He repeatedly referred to the place as "Grand Central *Terminal*," emphasizing the last word, and was militant about its being a *terminal* and not a *station*. The *terminal*, he told us, was built in the beaux arts style by the architectural firm of Reed and Stern. It remained, he said, the largest train *terminal* in the world, if you go by the number of platforms.

"Forty-four platforms," the young man said, "with sixty-seven tracks along them on two levels, forty-one on the upper one and twenty-six on the lower one. Every day, six hundred sixty Metro-North commuter trains cross the *terminal*, carrying about 125,000 commuters."

I smiled. Already, I was thinking of my grandfather. Did I remember him at just that moment because of the young man's mania for reciting trivia from memory? Or was the story of the Redstone trying to prick through my layers of consciousness?

The young man walked to the center of the station and we followed.

"This," he said, his voice echoing a little in the cavernous space, "is the Main Concourse. As you may have heard, we just finished a $250 million renovation, a large part of which went to cleaning up and restoring this magnificent ceiling." We all followed his pointer, craning our necks to look up.

"If you would have been here fifteen years ago, you would not have been able to see this ceiling. It was covered in thick dark grime. Can any of you guess what it was?"

"Diesel," said a huge man near the front.

Idiot, I thought. If the answer was an obvious one, the young man wouldn't have asked it.

"Nope," the young man said, satisfied.

"Cooking smoke," someone else said.

"Nope."

After this, people seemed to grow tired of the game. The young man scanned the group one more time and, perhaps sensing a mutiny, answered the question himself: "Cigarette smoke."

A murmur went through the gathered Americans, already sufficiently informed about the dirty deeds smoking does to one's lungs.

"We were able to restore the ceiling to almost its original colors," the young man said. This cozy "we" irritated me. Obviously, he hadn't been on the team of art preservationists, and the familiarity was out of line. But I let it pass.

"We left this part here untouched for comparison," he said. His laser circled a muddy patch above.

The big man near the front spoke up, maybe to ease his embarrassment over his earlier know-it-all tone.

"Who painted the original ceiling?"

"Excellent question." The guide smiled at the huge man. "He was a French artist named Paul César Helleu. Those of you who are astronomy buffs may notice a slight anomaly here." He paused very briefly but then continued. Clearly, he had decided to drop the question-and-answer routine with this crowd. He took out his laser and spanned the cosmos with it. "The sky," he said, "is backward."

Another intake of breath from the group.

"Pretty wild, no? We speculate that Helleu had taken for his model a medieval manuscript. Some of these star maps were drawn not from what would have been an earthly perspective, but from a heavenly one. At any rate, the peculiar perspective was too expensive to fix and so it stayed. I kind of like it myself."

The man in the front, grown unbearably obsequious now, heartily agreed.

"Now if we pass Aries and go here to Pisces," the young man continued, "those of you with good eyesight might notice a small dark patch. This is not tobacco smoke. It's actually a hole."

He waited a moment as people strained to see the void contained in the frenetic red circle.

"In 1957, the government brought in a missile to display," he said. "But they couldn't hoist it into place—the ceiling was too low. So a hole had to be cut. We decided, during the renovations, not to close it, since the hole, too, was part of history."

My heart beat suddenly. "A Redstone missile?" I asked.

The young man looked at me coolly. "Yes, ma'am, I believe it was a Redstone."

The others turned to look at me.

I nodded and smiled, though I could hear the blood in my ears. "My grandfather was a hobbyist." The young man's face seemed to relax. "We get a lot of them coming here to look at it," he said. "Older men, war buffs." He smiled and turned briskly on his feet. He moved with a light agility that suggested training. I guessed he was an aspiring actor.

"War buffs," I repeated. It sounded benign, a phrase from a gentler time, like some kind of Eisenhower-era cleaning product.

Our ideas about war follow the fashions. I got the sense that for this gathered crowd, as for me, the Redstone stunt was a kind of unbearable kitsch. Of course, in less than a year, war and missiles would acquire yet another meaning for New Yorkers. For Grandfather, who died not four months after the Berlin Wall fell, the only guilt about his work would have come from a feeling of not doing enough. Certainly one could argue that those who worked on the Redstone had to believe in the nobility of their service or else kill themselves with self-loathing and regret. But I think these are pretty weak explanations, rooted as they are in popular psychology. For Grandfather, and I suppose for many others like him, it was not a matter of justification or superficial causality. It was much deeper—a philosophical understanding, you could call it (perhaps instilled through osmosis from their German colleagues), of destruction as fine art. For Grandfather, war was not a catastrophe to be avoided but an aesthetic to be mastered, a discipline with its own nuances and rules. I can almost picture his wonder as he watched his Redstones blast off and pierce the sky, free, untethered, not subject to the normal laws of gravity or common sense. In the end, the Grand Central Redstone—inert and impotent—must have appeared ridiculous to him, too, though for different reasons entirely.

I heard the tour guide as if from far off. "And we come now to this exquisite marble pagoda," he was saying. "It has a secret . . ."

But I remained there in the middle of the concourse, face turned up to the confused cosmos, its pinpricked void.

Perhaps you have experienced this yourself: the vertigo that takes hold when you stare too long and too far into an indeterminate height. The noise of the platform fell away and the earth tilted to the stars, but still I could not look away from that dark wound.

The Express
BY MARTA YARA BALDWIN

The rain had been falling for two days, a steady beat in the dull-metal autumn of those parts, and Marta was glad to be inside the safety of the moving train. She had brought work with her but had already spent the first half hour of the commute watching the landscape go by, mesmerized by the blurred shapes in shades of gray—trees, village houses, cars. Now and then an umbrella shielded a solitary figure. Others might have found in this scene a melancholy strain, but for Marta it brought an unexpected peace. She was dry inside her compartment, and warm. It occurred to her that she was happy. Not happy in the way she had been as a young woman, when her future glittered before her and she had mistaken the intoxicating newness of the world for love. Then, she had gladly flung herself into the abyss for her beloved, annihilated herself in his embrace. In those days, she had let all the terror and exhilaration of the unknown soak her like a sudden rain. No, not happy in that way. Happy in what Marta understood now was an honest happiness, an enduring sense of contentment that arose from the everyday. She liked to say that the big-ticket pleasures—the weddings, the fine jobs, the grand gestures—had too many moving parts. True happiness was this, being conducted through the wet, forbidding countryside, sheltered in a metal cocoon. She was grateful to the engineers, the designers, the countless workers who had ensured that her trip would be a pleasant one.

She was grateful, too, that she had made the transition to middle age with a minimum of drama. There had been tears, a big disappointment, the sense of having failed at the one thing that mattered. But then had come understanding and a second chance. She knew now that happiness was not the big house, but the orderly kitchen; not the excitement of the chase, but the calm endurance. She took pleasure in her post at the university and even in the two-hour commute that shuttled her between work and home. As a young woman she would have fought and railed against the distance, but she knew enough now to accept and even look forward to the long ride. Those hours in motion were often the only time she had to herself these days and she welcomed the solitude, the gentle rocking familiarity of the train, and the landscape that changed with mood and season and yet managed to remain the same. She made the trip three times a week, and three times a week her husband and young son waited for her, dinner steaming on the stove.

Marta leaned back in her chair. The first-class compartment was nearly empty, even though it was close to the rush hour now. A man a few seats down coughed, and then there was no sound except for the occasional rustle of his paper and the steady chug chug of the train. Marta watched the gray landscape, the train's motion rocking her in and out of light sleep. Now and then she woke with the sense that she should attend to her papers, but she allowed herself to sink into the delicious laziness of work deferred. They arrived at the halfway station. The train always waited here a few extra minutes to absorb commuters arriving from other parts. On the platform, men in dark suits walked quickly in all directions, eyes focused on the timetables. Three teenage boys lingered by the newsstand, where an older woman, wearing a pink hat and white gloves, was buying a magazine. A rowdy group of girls entered the first-class compartment, sat down, and then quickly abandoned their seats amid a riot of giggles. All these people: how extraordinary it seemed that Marta would never know any of them, would probably never see them again. Was this normal? It seemed all of them—herself included—moved through the world as spectators now. Certainly this was a new phenomenon in the history of humanity. Five thousand years ago, how many strangers would an average woman encounter? How many unfamiliar faces, anonymous lives? Probably none, Marta decided. This commonplace fact suddenly struck her as profoundly unsettling. What was the purpose of all this . . . life? This hurrying about among people she didn't know? The whistle blew and the train began to pull out. As it slowly swept the platform, Marta's eyes settled on a bench near the station's edge. A woman sat there alone. As the train approached her with advancing speed, the woman's face came into focus and Marta saw that she was crying. And then, just as quickly, the platform fell away and the familiar landscape returned. Marta's unease left her as quickly as it had arrived. Moving through the open land again, she relaxed; her calm contentment returned. Her husband had cautioned her about what he called her thinking problem. And Marta knew that he was right. She was always happiest when she didn't think, didn't allow ruminations. Her life was peaceful and she was happy.

The sun's light was fading. Every day, darkness came earlier. Soon, she would leave the university at twilight and pass through the countryside at night. Now the darkening landscape outside the window included a faint mirror image of Marta's face in the glass. She turned away and settled her head to nap. She would get to the papers when she was fresh, tomorrow morning. The train's movement lulled her. She didn't know how long she had slept before she woke suddenly to the sound of brakes. The whistle blowing wildly. The train slowed, but didn't stop. Then the sound of debris hitting the undercarriage. Ping, ping. Bits of wood and concrete. Maybe glass shards. Some wreck on the tracks. Finally the train stopped. The smell of smoking metal reached the first-class compartment. Marta waited for an announcement. The rain fell against the glass, beading into small streams. She cupped her face to the window. Outside, the darkened countryside. There wasn't enough light to help her make out where they were. She checked her clock. About half an hour from town. Marta stood. She was alone in her compartment. In the next, a group of people sat, gesturing to one another. She walked to the front, opened the door, and leaned in. "What happened?" she asked.

"No idea," said a man.

"We hit something," said his companion.

Marta nodded and walked back to her seat. She sat and waited. Surely there would be an announcement. After ten minutes of more silence, she called her husband.

"Something's happened on the tracks," she said, "and we're just stopped here. Eat without me." She could hear her son chatting in the background. He was almost four, and had reached the age when words and their arrangement must seem a magical wonder. He talked constantly now, mixing questions with statements, moving from curiosity to grandiosity and back again on an endless stream of sound. In solitude, he continued to talk, issuing emphatic appeals to imaginary boys who might share their trains, or counting wildly, endlessly. The life in him was that strong. Marta sometimes had to tune him out, and afterward she always felt guilty.

After a while, the loudspeaker crackled and Marta waited for the conductor's voice. But there was only the sound of feedback and then nothing. This happened a few more times before the conductor finally spoke.

"Ladies and gentlemen, there has been an accident on the tracks. We will be making an announcement shortly."

The conductor thanked the passengers for their cooperation, as if commuters were always on the verge of mutiny and must be periodically appeased with soothing words or fresh coffee. In fact, it was all the opposite, Marta realized now. How docile they all were, how willing to be shepherded from one point to the other, with few demands, with almost infinite understanding. All the rage they might have shown behind their own steering wheels was sublimated when they were passengers. They had become little children, relinquishing their own fate. Marta waited. Someone came through the compartment quickly, and then it was quiet again. She dozed. A whistle sounded. Or sirens. The train lurched forward a few feet and then stopped. Marta opened her eyes and looked at her watch. Two hours. She stood to stretch. Outside, night had fallen. The rain continued harder now. What could possibly be keeping them?

Marta took her wallet and went into the dining car. It was full, with barely enough room to stand. Everyone had come here, and the din of voices after so much silence momentarily disoriented her. She made her way to the counter and ordered a coffee. A young man handed her a plastic cup and when their fingers touched she asked him what had happened. Before he could answer, a woman standing behind her said, "Suicide."

Marta turned around quickly. "Suicide?"

The other woman nodded. She pressed her hands together and sighed. "That's what they're saying."

Marta turned back to the man behind the counter. He shrugged. "No idea, myself."

"Suicide," the woman repeated. "Guy just stood on the tracks and waited for it. That's what they're saying."

Marta returned to her seat. She opened the lid of her coffee to let it cool. Then she took a sip. Black and bitter. She took another sip. After a long while, the train began to move. The loudspeaker cracked.

"Ladies and gentlemen, as you can see, we're on our way again. Quite a sad incident on the tracks this afternoon. It happens now at least twice a month. Usually, like today, it's a young man. They appear at the last minute, knowing we won't be able to stop. A terrible tragedy. Terrible."

He paused as if he wanted to add something. But then the loudspeaker went cold. After a few minutes, the train picked up speed through the countryside. The familiar rocking. Marta picked up her phone, began to dial, and then shut it. She sat back and listened to the rolling wheels. The sound of glass hitting the undercarriage. The ping of debris. It had been shattered bone. What she'd heard was the broken hard skeleton of life.

All she could see now in the window was her own reflection; the landscape beyond dissolved in night and rain. God is less free than man because He cannot kill Himself if He wanted to. Where had she read that? As a graduate student, all those years ago, when the force of living seemed too much to bear. She sat for a moment, chilled. And then she realized that she could understand this young man, understand how close happiness lies to the precipice. Not peace. Peace lives in a different country. Bliss and despair alone share the void. To be so full of longing for the high joys of this life that the music roars even within the lasting silence. She had felt all those things once. She had flown higher than she thought possible, felt the world come together and fall away beneath her feet. Her bruised return was part of the gift. So much feeling compressed into a tight life. And now? Now she was whole, complete, content. She breathed and loved.

She'd banished danger; but never again would she be invited to dance on its electric rim.

It was past nine P.M. when the train pulled into the station. The rain fell hard, and Marta waited a long time for a cab. She sat in silence through the emptied streets of their town. Everything recognizable and yet newly made. Why must there be signs and curbs and lights that switch from red to green? Was this really the best of all possible worlds, or were there others, just beyond our reach? Outside her house, she paid the fare and stood on the sidewalk as the cab pulled away.

Rain fell in cold white sheets now, but Marta did not move. The curtains in her house were open. In the warm yellow light of the living room sat her husband and child. Their faces were turned away, but now and then their heads moved and Marta could see they were laughing. She stood there a long time, letting the rain sink through her coat, her sweater, letting it soak straight through to the warm center of her still-beating self.

Zodiac of Loss
BY JOHNNY ALDO

Ram: Running, running, always running. You think this way you will find it, but this thing—this non-consonant you long for—burrows out of sight, stays still, and waits in shadow. You cannot disturb his flight, not in this story.

Taurus: Victory is not in your cards, you with your bull-mind, always looking but failing to find. This non-consonant runs from you, too. Vanquish longing and ambition if you wish to abandon your rough body and fly.

Twins: Why should you miss anything? You who split in two so as to vanish at our last hour, abandoning that non-you who stains this psalm with ink. Dying was always your solution to sorrow.

Crab: Tomorrow, with luck, tomorrow this sand will shift and you will drag your body to a spot that will show you all is not lost. Crawling mystic, only you can point our way; only you know how to cast off this shroud of stars.

Lion: Far from your savanna, you roam now, having cast your lot with this world's most solitary spirits. You think this is a sort of victory, but it is a hollow kind. What you miss is missing still, and you also will not find it.

Virgo: Wit and glamour follow you; sun rays light your path. Your days flow without drama and nights fall soft, with nothing lost. But this missing non-consonant haunts you, too. You cannot think a thing without choking on its sorrowful half. And truth is always out of hand, always far, too far to hold.

Libra: Bold and warm sun sign, you kiss young crops and pray for growth. Ubiquitous as rain you fall, calm and fair, upon this land. But you, too, long for that missing spark; you, too, wish for this chaos that no human soul can long contain.

Scorpio: Fountains of poison flow from your body, but you pay no mind to sorrow. Passion is your spirit's only truth, play its only aim. So you miss not as much; you claim to long for nothing. Still, this thing that you call "no" runs from you at night.

Sagittarius: Lighting wax pillars, you banish night. Without drama or too much laughing, curious and happy, you roam a domain of possibility. Not for you this look-looking without finish. Not for you to fill your mouth with sour longing. That which is lost can stay that way. It is nothing to you.

Capricorn: Too swift you run, ram of January. All this running will thwart you also, most unsmiling of signs. Truth is found in small mounds of dirt, not in mountains. It is that which you cannot knock down, that which falls to no fight. Now, trim your horns and sit down to pray.

Aquarius: Day finds you dynamic and loquacious, night shy and withdrawn. So it is with you, liquid god of duality. You do not know what to do about our missing non-consonant. By day, you wish it found at last. By night, you wish it always lost. But your complicity is not an option: you must, in light or dark, still look. It is your duty, too.

Fish: You swim throughout this book, splashing into conscious mind now and again. Silly fish, slim ghost of that which cannot solitary grow. You look and look, longing for proof of a vast liquid cosmos containing all you cannot touch, all that your soul says is missing and will stay missing. And still, you can swim without it. Only you do not know it.

Journey Back to the Seed
(¿Qué Quieres, Vieja?)
BY ALEX CARPENTER

I

In the end, she is surrounded by strangers. She dreams of returning to the sea and wakes every evening in a new house to find the bed is floating in a different ocean. The hallway outside the room where she stays sometimes twists to the right, sometimes to the left, and sometimes there is no right or left, no sometimes only this moment, no hallway at all, just a thick whiteness that she steps into, falling and stumbling until she begins to swim to the light.

II

One of the strangers takes her by the hand. He is talking very quickly, and she can't understand his mumbling. He is pulling her into a room. But who is the old woman he screams about? She herself is only fourteen years old. Who is this man trying to harm her? Pedro Sosa, Pedro Sosa, somebody help me Pedro Sosa is trying to harm me. He's lost his mind. A door she never noticed before opens and a woman appears. She is beautiful, talking softly, and even though there is no understanding what she says, it's clear that she has come to help. The man lets go of her. The woman leads her to a new bed, in a different room. This house is endless, like a honeycomb, backward and forward mean the same. That's it, that's it. What ugly furniture. This isn't her house. She will close her eyes again. When she closes her eyes, night comes and her aunt Caridad comes to visit her, slipping through the blinds with the moonlight. Today I wrote a new poem, she tells her aunt Caridad. And I recited it in front of all the school. The other students applauded and applauded. I'm going to be a writer, she tells Caridad. And her aunt Caridad caresses her long hair as she's always done.

At that indistinct time that is neither morning nor night, her son wakes in the next room. He has heard something. What suffering, at his age, to have an ill mother. What bad luck his whole life. All the struggling, the hardships he endured. Leaving the university at nineteen to come to this country, leaving his education, working day and night to pay for his parents' passage. And now his mother doesn't know his own name.

Don't go away, she pleads with her aunt Caridad. Don't go away, don't go away, don't go away, don't go away, don't go away, don't go away.

III

Today a pretty girl gives her a kiss. You are very pretty, she tells the girl. I don't want you to become a flirt, or a whore. Don't become a whore. The pretty girl laughs, though this is a very serious affair. She worries about these pretty girls. This one especially, with the short skirt and the blouse that looks like underclothes. Don't be a whore, don't be a whore, or a flirt.

Don't be a flirt. My aunt Caridad, yes, my aunt Caridad's a mess, this pretty girl has a curl, my aunt Caridad, no, my aunt Caridad knows.

Don't go away! Don't go away! Don't go away!

Ah no, but here comes Pedro Sosa with the bad news. Get away from me Pedro Sosa. I don't want to know. My beautiful mother. And with five children.

She is so hungry now. She hasn't eaten in years. She sits quietly. They lie to her, telling her she has already eaten. It is terrible to be a child. Her father is returning from the countryside. She is wearing her best clothes. There was a storm overnight, but the weather is good now. The weather is good now so there is nothing to worry about.

Another pretty girl walks by. She reaches for her, Tell me, whose house is this?

IV

Don't go away, don't go away, don't go away, this is my house, this is not my house, Pedro Sosa, no, the house of Caridad, no, the house of Esther, no, the house of Cuca, yes, don't go away, don't go away, there is nothing to eat today, nothing to eat in Cuca's house, Pedrito, no, Lita, no, the house of Caridad, yes, and there is nothing to eat today in my mother's house. She has spent the entire morning like that, the daughter-in-law tells her daughters. Conjuring up all the dead. Wandering the house like a soul in purgatory.

V

This new house is full of unfamiliar people. An old woman passes. What did I do to deserve this punishment? she asks. The old woman doesn't respond. I don't like old women, she tells her. The old woman laughs. And you, what are you? New, white-orange shoes? Chew, will you Jew? Not Jewish, Jewish, Jewish. Methodist. My mother, the house of Caridad. She sits back in an unfamiliar sofa. Why am I here? It's very simple, the old woman responds, your daughter doesn't want you in the house anymore.

How could she have a daughter when she is only fifteen years old? Everyone is confused. O God, she prays, give me strength, my father is dead and they have brought me to a madhouse. In the library, far away, beyond anything the woman can hear or understand, two young women talk in whispers. Memory marks and makes us. Not intelligence, it's not that. For a beast, every morning is new; the past is oblivion. Only man looks back, caresses his gathered history as if it were a beloved parent. Without memory there would be no hate, no accumulated wrongs, no learning, no love. Look at her; without memory there is only the dulling wind of words.

VI

His sister is crying, hysterical. I can't take it anymore, she screams. Twenty years she's lived with me. Twenty years. I'm an old woman myself. I can't endure it anymore. She can't stay here. She tries to torment me, she is fine, there's nothing wrong with her, only she's trying to torment me. I can't endure it. Why does it have to always be me? All the suffering I've passed through, and before that our father. Both of them living here for years and years. It's your turn now. I can't bear this hardship.

And she leaves her brother's house with her mother in the seat next to her and drives backward through the streets.

In her daughter's house, in the first darkness, she is most afraid. I haven't died, I haven't died. You listening there, can you tell me if I've died yet? Have you? How can you be sure? What a curse this is, that she can find nothing at all with which to sweeten her last days.

VII

In the street, a boy bids her farewell. She presses a gold ring into his hand. Take it, she says. For him. You must know my dear late husband. Know him, he is my closest neighbor, but he is very bad off these days. The woman blinks and opens her eyes. This boy has come from the other side. I know, the old woman says. He is named Laika—his parents loved everything Soviet, but they didn't know about the name until it was too late. Better a victorious canine than a capitalist slave. She watches him ascend to heaven, over the ocean, on a single white wing. When she tells the others about this, no one believes her.

VIII

The woman rises, takes off her robe and her sleeping gown, puts in her hearing aid and her teeth. Someone helps her, buttons her blouse. There, there, time to go to sleep, Mother, the confused woman tells her. Out of pity, she walks out to the front yard with this woman. It is still dark, but she can see the red in the sky, the sun rising. After, she goes inside to breakfast on black beans. This is a strange house. But she eats because she is very hungry. She sits to wait for the school bus. Hello, the woman says as she closes the door, and takes her by the hand to lead her from the house. Good-bye, they tell her on the school bus as she climbs in for the ride back to school. She is happy at the school, with all her friends. Sometimes she has to shove that boy who irritates her, but usually she is a good girl. Yesterday, as tomorrow, she dances with a black man that she likes very much, but she must be careful not to tell anyone. After ice cream and pizza, she becomes very tired, until they give her some pills that restore her energy. Then they put her on the bus again. Hello, the driver tells her as she gets off the bus. Good-bye, the woman says at the door of the house where she has just arrived.

She sits down to a hurried dinner of milky coffee and bread. And now—but how could she have missed it? This is her daughter sitting across from her. The poor thing, how she's aged in such a short time. Of course, I'm fine, she tells her daughter. Stop screaming, for God's sake. I just didn't realize I was still here.

IX

Slowly, imperceptibly, she begins to remember. Little things at first, so it is no problem. It is nothing she worries about. Not yet. In the middle of a conversation, the pleasant stranger she was talking to will turn out to be her grandson. She will open her mouth to complain about the food and suddenly remember that her daughter has an ill temper.

One day she pulls a piece of paper from her pocket. She sits down at a table to read:

> My name is Marina.
>
> I was married for fifty years before my husband died. Now I am a widow.
>
> I live with my daughter and her husband.
>
> Sometimes I become disoriented, remembering people I've never known.
>
> I have three children, named after myself and the saints. My six grandchildren are named after the stars: Sirius, Canopus, Centauri, Arcturus, Vega, Capella.

Before she is finished reading, she goes over everything again, beginning at the end, until all the words are back inside the pen with which she both writes and erases.

X

The days and years begin to pass more quickly. Before, when every day was new and there was only the present minute, time meant nothing and everything. An entire world was contained in one second and the dead could cross the membrane of space to hold her hand. She spent hundreds of years this way, and fleeting seconds also. Now that she remembers more and more, the days are elastic, continuous; long in all the wrong places and short where they matter most. The old confusion is passing, little by little the world is making sense, but something else is lost. She has to remember now that she will give her husband the pills between afternoon and morning. She has to think now about what she will do when her children become babies. When the twins are born and they have so little money.

XI

The time has finally come when they can leave America for home. Now little by little Marina will forget her English, until she doesn't know that she needs it anymore. She and her husband take their tattered coats and used jeans and leave them at the church, rifling through the boxes, jostling the others, so they can bury the best clothes at the bottom of the pile before the others see them.

At the airport, the soldiers return the bracelet that her mother gave her before she died. They tear up the false bottoms of their suitcases and put in all their old diplomas, the marriage certificate, the photographs, and the newspaper clippings. The soldiers take dollars out of their own pockets and tear up the soles of her shoes so they can stuff them with money before closing them again with the slash of a knife.

At home, trembling, she stitches back the bottom of the suitcase, takes the shoes to a man they have told her about so that he can unstitch them. Then she carefully unfolds the dollars hidden there and hides them in her brassiere.

That morning she cannot think with fear, a long abiding

fear such as she's never known, as if her thoughts, whatever it is that she is, were coming apart, expanding through space, leaving her with the thinnest thread of her body's understanding. Before she closes her eyes to undo all her dreaming, she is troubled with a deep sadness. She tries and tries to make sense of it, but cannot be sure if her unease is a suppressed memory or a premonition of terror to come.

XII

One afternoon, out in the fields, it seems to her that the sun is crawling back up the sky toward the east. If it sinks below the ridgeline, she thinks, nothing will ever be certain again.

XIII

The seasons pass as before. The wind changes. Her children grow more and more dull until their ignorance becomes a great physical discomfort. And then that, too, dissipates and she can no longer remember what it was like to be so burdened by hardship and obligation. All endured sufferings pass. On a cool, beautiful day in October, her husband hires musicians and invites her family and his to a celebration on the beach. Marina watches the waves as they shorten to grace the shore and then pull back long and high again into the deep ocean. At the church, a priest takes back what he's said word by word, until he is standing before them, his hand raised over their heads in silence. Her husband takes her by the hand, and with the soft chaste touch of his cheek on hers, returns her to her old widowed mother.

Marina has never been happier. She thinks she could live for years and years and still never be so happy.

XIV

Now that her husband has renounced his dominion over her, she begins to write poetry, discovering words in the stove, forming sentences out of the ashes.

> *My name is Marina I am*
> *Who sits down to write who*
> *Am I who writes*
> *Night's*
> *Golden thoughts.*

Her sad, sick mother begins to improve as Marina's own thought becomes more and more feeble. The fewer medicines the doctors give her mother, the faster she recovers. By the time the last doctor leaves, Marina's mother is well again, with nothing more than a small pain in her back to remind her of her illness. And to think I died so many years ago, she says to her daughter, who can no longer order her words with the old ease, to whom death now seems as distant and unreal as a forgotten self.

XV

A terrible storm comes from worlds away, so obscene and unnatural that thunder precedes lightning. In the periodic brilliance that lights the countryside, the rain—for a fleeting moment—seems to be falling to heaven.

I remember, she thinks, that this is the night I lose my father. And no sooner has she finished the thought than despair gives way to hope. All the ghosts are out tonight, her mother says. And me with five children to care for. Together they sit at the window and watch as the limping figure of Pedro Sosa becomes smaller and smaller in the distance, until he vanishes like a gnarled dream into the rain.

XVI

The time of books and pens and paper passes. She spends her days close to the ground now, listening for footsteps. The white tile floor is endless. It takes years to crawl from one end of the house to another. Cuca's house is dark and cool. One of her aunts picks her up and sits her on a sofa. She stays, unable to make out what is being said to her. She raises her arms and lets them fall. Another aunt picks her up and begins to bounce her. There is nothing she can do about this. She sleeps. She wakes hungry and tries to speak of it, but cannot. She lies still in a bed that she does not recognize, until the door opens and her mother, her sweet mother, lifts her to her face. My dear mother, the last and first face I see, don't go away from here, don't go away and leave me all alone.

XVII

In the beginning, she is surrounded by strangers, without a face to recognize or a memory to soothe her. She has lost even the understanding of language and lies helpless, sobbing, without knowing the meaning of sadness. The pleasure of the body turning through space, the sound of wind moving counterclockwise through the emptiness—all forgotten. Exquisite fingers she no longer remembers how to use, legs that once paddled through a warm dark sea. And then her soul passing through a pinhole in the firmament, her thin thread-self forgetting that she had once remembered the pleasure of the body, the sound of the wind . . . Nameless now she goes, tearing stars into time's shroud, cleansed and purified for the journey's return.

The Boy Who Fell from Heaven

BY LAIKA ALMEIDA

June 4, 1969: Armando Socarras Ramirez and Jorge Perez Blanco climb into the right landing gear well of an Iberia DC-8, Flight 904 from Havana, Cuba, to Madrid, Spain. Socarras survives the flight with severe shock and exposure. Initially it is thought Perez fell from the aircraft during flight, either during a secondary retraction to clear a warning light, or during landing preparation, as Socarras indicates he spoke to Perez during some duration of the flight. Later he claims that Perez attempted to climb into the left well and failed, and he believes Perez is in a Cuban prison.

August 12, 2000: Roberto Viza Egües hides himself in an Air France cargo container in Havana, Cuba, and arrives in Paris, France, the following day suffering from exposure but otherwise in good condition. France eventually denies his application for asylum based on lack of evidence of persecution, and deports him back to Cuba.

Christmas Eve, 2000: Sixteen-year-old Maikel Almira and fifteen-year-old Alberto Rodriguez climb into the wheel wells of a British Airways 777 in Havana, Cuba.

Almira's body is found in a field five miles from Gatwick Airport in England. Rodriguez's body falls from the aircraft the following day as it departs for a flight to Cancún, Mexico. Almira had left a note for his mother suggesting he was going to the United States. However, the departure of a Miami-bound flight had been delayed and the flight to Gatwick took over its slot.[8]

April Fools' Day, 2009: Seventeen-year-old Laika Almeida climbs into the wheel well of an American Airlines Boeing 737 in Havana, Cuba. On the plane's approach to Miami, some passengers report seeing an object falling from the bottom of the plane. Later, others claim it was an enormous bird.

As soon as he was about ten feet from the water, he sliced the strings. The chute shot up, folded violently on itself, and crumpled like a blown white jellyfish. A second later, he splashed down. He took off his flight suit, let it float away, and stripped to swimming trunks. The water was warm as a shroud of stars. He paddled in place for a while, letting it heat him, before turning to shore. He figured it took him half an hour to swim to the buoys. It was getting dark. He scanned the beach for the curious. But no one was looking in his direction. It was Saturday; the people were lined up on the sand. A summer day in June, now ending.

---

8. From http://en.wikipedia.org/wiki/Stowaway.

On the shore, two boys threw a ball between them, arguing and shouting. Laika watched them from the water. When they were gone, he walked out, dripping. He lay on the sand, letting the waning sun dry him, waiting for his beating heart to calm. What fear and what magnificence! To be soaring, then plunging, then the jerk of the chute, the falling, the splash. Gravitational laws not suspended, but engaged, the water yearning for him. That was it: the earth desired play, and we had mistaken its challenges for toil. The long ideology of human suffering. Laika longed to escape it. He fled not a place, but a condition. How to explain it, even to himself? It was as impossible and thrilling as escaping the need for breath.

Laika sat on the sand and waited, not knowing for what. After an hour, when the sun was beginning to set behind the buildings, a man and a woman arrived. They stopped a few paces from Laika and began to strip to their bathing suits. They ran to the water and dived in. Laika watched them swim out to the buoys. He was waiting for this. He strolled down the beach, put his legs into the man's khakis, reached into his white T-shirt, and slipped on his flip-flops. Then he kept walking. So easy, this assuming of another life. He was one of many now. No one looked at him. He walked west, following the sun. Apartment buildings and bars, a long and busy street. The cars so new, the street so wide and clean. He had traveled to the future on a nylon balloon. Who could argue otherwise with him? Sleek sleekness everywhere and the quiet of fine machinery. The little islands of green in the middle of the smooth asphalt. The palm trees that never offered shelter or shade. He crossed another road—a highway, really, or so it seemed to him—and came to a street of green plants and wide houses, what Miramar had been once, maybe. Teletransported to this future, this alternate Cuba where history went right instead of left. Flip-flops snapping happily, he walked to where? Two girls went by in a convertible. He followed the curve of the street, feeling only the asphalt beneath the thin rubber of the sandals, the breeze blown by the setting sun, an emptiness that was not yet hunger, only delicious anticipation. Ahead, an old woman in a long housecoat. Growing as Laika approaches. She sees him and her placid confusion turns to terror.

Pedro Sosa, she says.

Laika Almeida.

Pedro Sosa, she says.

Laika Almeida.

All the same, she says.

It is not all the same. Not at all.

Where are you from?

Me?

You. Did you fall from heaven?

Yes, that's it. I fell from heaven, he says. He is already close enough to the old woman to see the rings on her fingers, notice the red stones set in gold.

Heaven? Yes, I remember heaven, a heaven beyond the stars. You fell from heaven?

In a balloon.

I know that, the old woman says. Annoyed, now.

Pardon me, ma'am.

Heaven, is it? If you're really from heaven then you would know . . . you would know . . .

Your husband.

My husband, yes, you would know my dear husband. My dear . . . my dear . . .

I know many husbands in heaven. Would his name be Juan?

Juan! You know my dear Juan.

Know him? We are neighbors. But he is in a bad way, very poor.

Poor in heaven!

Ma'am, my apologies. There are poor in heaven and also rich. It is the same as earth, except without death.

To be poor with no hope of death! The old woman begins to cry. My poor Juan, who worked all his life, his life all struggle and tears and work.

Laika takes the woman's hand, the one with the rubies. My fair woman, I will tell him that you send your love.

My love! What good will my love do a poor man in heaven?

Laika lowers his eyes, fingers the bright rubies.

I know, the old woman says. Take this ring, of what use is it to me now? It will be far more valuable in heaven. Take it to Juan and tell him that it is now his wife's turn to care for him.

Laika bows low at the waist and takes the ring into his palm, holding it tight. You are a good and generous woman, he says. I will see to it that your husband receives your gift. He will be the happiest man in heaven.

The old woman smiles, all traces of her former terror gone. She turns and Laika watches her go. The ring will feed him for a time. In heaven, all things are possible.

He sleeps beneath a coconut palm that night. A man roams the dark beach, playing the violin. Another wakes him before dawn to warn him of the alien creatures hiding in the sea oats. The tides have swept in all the madmen, and Laika knows he's one of them.

~

In time, he finds work. Every morning, except Sunday, he rises early and takes a bus to the mainland. There, he meets the work crew and boards the trucks that will drive them to the day's site. Most days, they work on those islands of green in the middle of the highway, the islands that Laika has learned to call "medians." The others complain of the heat and the bosses, attached as they are to the ideology of suffering. But not Laika. He enjoys the spreading warmth of the sun. He likes the way the weed-eater vibrates in his hand. Likes even the name "weed-eater," as if it were some voracious half-animal on a visit from the future. The lion's roar of the mower, the sweet smell of diesel, the sweat of honest industry. Even as the cars speed past, drivers oblivious, Laika rejoices. It is as if he is watching time itself always moving, moving with great mechanical displacements of air, while he prunes the ixora.

He has tried to get the other men to understand what he has learned. We are not just landscapers; we are the restorers of order, the last line against chaos. Where would this humid, decaying city be without us? The grass would cover more and more of the earth, seeds blown by the wind. The roots of big trees would spread, slowly insinuating themselves beneath the concrete sidewalks, the black asphalt, gently, imperceptibly displacing road and alleyway, every day throwing up small shards of rock until the cracks extended from one end of the city to another. The hibiscus would choke the rose. The invasive pines would smother the natives. In only a few years, the city would be returned to green. Water would collect in the damaged streets, in the trunks of putrifying palms, and the mosquitoes would return, black swarms thick enough to choke a man. They always laughed when he spoke like this. They began to call him the Prophet. But they were all misfits in one way or another, men who, like everyone else, had begun their adult lives with great hopes and stumbled somewhere. Many had been in jail; others were illegals—"without the proper papers" "undocumented" "exploited" "capitalist outcasts." It was natural that they should view their work as hard labor, as punishment for their lives. It was the way they had been taught to view the vicissitudes of this life. From Genesis to the stations of the cross, their cosmos was one of pain. But Laika was none of these things. He was a boy who had fallen from heaven. He was on a great and mortal adventure.

Laika took an apartment by the beach. Every afternoon, when he returned, he walked into the ocean in his work clothes, bits of leaves and twigs floating away from his body. When the wind was good, he sat on the shore and watched the men who came to surf the waves, tethered to a giant kite. He would look at them and think of his own strange journey, the billow of nylon and the strings he had cut forever.

The afternoon of the parachute seemed so far away. He missed nothing, not his home, not his dear parents. Neither did he understand the insistence of people on knowing the details of his biography. Where was he born? How old was he? What were his parents' names? Was his childhood happy? Did he have a mango tree? Eat black beans? Laika didn't understand why these things should be important at all. He was amused at people's need for lists and attributes. One day, a woman reading in the park asked him what his *motivation* was. These kinds of questions bored him. When he told the woman so, she huffed and said, under her breath, What a character! He was not a *character*; he did not suffer from motivations or ancient traumas. He wanted nothing, not even to complain. Neither did he understand the men in the work crew, always arguing about one or another point of history, prodding him to say what he really thought of Cuba, give the reasons why he left. Laika understood that they wanted him to express some certainty that eluded them. It eluded him too, but he was at peace with it. Why had he left? There were no reasons and an infinite number of them, but he could not list them for the men. To do so would consume their entire lives; and what would they understand anyway of flight? Their notions of escape were of the crudest kind. Laika's were as tiny and joyful as Lucretius's clinamen. He was happy to leave them inexpressible and ungraspable.

In December of that year, the ficus around Miami began to die. First the leaves turned yellow, then they fell off. The dense green hedges that had ringed the city's finest homes vanished, as if someone had pulled down a haughty woman's skirt. Hard dry skeletons stood in their place. At first, the owners blamed the work crews, accused them of spreading too much poison. Laika defended himself as well as he could. But soon it emerged that the culprit was the fig whitefly (and because such things seem mandatory in stories such as these, we will give its scientific name: *Singhiella simplex*). Laika loved her right away.

Whiteflies are small and winged. They are pale, as their name implies, though not quite white. Their entrance into south Florida seems to have caught everyone by surprise. They are often described as "nonnative," though Laika supposed this meant they flew in from somewhere no one could name. They are clever and industrious. They live on the shady side of leaves, feeding like any other living thing. But the powers called them invasive pests and raised an alarm. The owners of all those beautiful ficus began to arm themselves for the invasion. This struck Laika as even more absurd than questions about his motivations. Wasn't every homeowner an invasive pest to his own patch of land? Had he not attached himself to it, bled it of nutrients? It was one thing to be a bulwark against chaos, to trim back the living so all might coexist. But it was another to single out a creature much like oneself and mark it for destruction. It seemed to Laika that the city and its people had gone mad.

One morning shortly after the new year, at the work crew's meeting, Laika and the others were briefed on new contingency plans. That's what the managers called it. Laika didn't know what contingency meant and had to wait for one of the workers to explain it to him. Immediately, he grew suspicious. The manager's plans included soaking the roots of ficus plants with a chemical whose name Laika couldn't remember, no matter how he tried (it was imidacloprid, and it's marketed by a certain maker of aspirin) All Laika understood was the label on the bottle, "Advanced Garden Tree and Shrub Control." There was nothing in there about the whitefly. If pressed, Laika would have to admit that he had nothing against chemicals. His reaction against the contingency plans was more romantic. In the battle between the ficus and the whitefly, his heart was with the fly. Miami had too many ficus anyway. They had grown proud and obnoxious in their ubiquity. If only this chemical contingency could live up to its name and control the shrubs, then Laika would happily help spread it. But he knew that the contingency plans—as the managers said—had been drawn up to save the ficus at the expense of the whitefly. For two weeks, while his colleagues spread the poison in the medians and across the elegant lawns of Miami, Laika stayed away. He didn't take the early bus to meet the work crews. And when his cell phone rang, he didn't pick it up. Instead, he took long walks in South Beach, noting the bare, brown skeletons ringing so many apartment buildings. Once, he shook a sturdy still-green shrub and stood back as hundreds of whiteflies flew out, as if he had blown on a dandelion. In the evenings, he swam out to the buoys and watched the sun set, far back over the city. Sometimes, he re-created his first walk, going as far as the elegant neighborhood—now he knew it was called Bay Road—to see if he might meet the old woman of the ruby ring again. One time, he met a man walking a yellow Labrador; another time, two young women out for a jog. But he never again saw the old woman.

At the start of the third week, Laika decided he needed to get rid of his money. Having few vices, he had managed to save up quite a bit. The first thing he did was pay out the rest of the contract on his studio. Then he went to a shop run by two French brothers, Queneau and Perec, where he bought a board and an iridescent golden kite and signed up for lessons. He set aside enough of the remaining money to buy himself a month's worth of crepes at A La Folie. It was February and the wind was cooperative. Laika finished his lessons in less than two weeks. By that time, the ficus were already coming back.

But Laika never returned to lawn maintenance. He spent every afternoon out on the water, not even missing the hum of the weed-eater. His hands controlled a greater force now, a thing visible only in the billowing of his kite. He approached kite-surfing the same way he had approached landscaping, with the slow, methodical concentration of a monk. He woke just before dawn and walked to the beach with his equipment. There he would work until it was light, patiently spreading out the lines, smoothing errant tangles, restoring order before blowing up the bladders and checking the harness. He could always count on an early morning jogger to launch him. And then he waded out to the water, giving the signal to let go the golden kite. He would slip his feet in the toeholds and wait for the wind to take him. Then it was like a giant engine revving and in seconds he was skimming the surface of the water, everything quiet except for the slap slap of the board.

He continued in this way, each day growing stronger than the day before. Then one day, at the beginning of May, Laika put his last dollar in his pocket, as a souvenir, and went down to the beach with his kite. Others were already there, setting up on the sand. There was good northeast wind blowing, about twenty knots. Laika was glad he had brought his twelve. He exchanged some pleasantries with the others. He liked the kiters, their easy humor. No one asked too many questions. No one wanted to know your motivations, where you came from, where you were going. They just wanted to ride. Another kiter launched him. Laika looped around the beach a few times, did some tricks for the people watching on the shore. Then he adjusted the kite. Nothing now but the sound of his board in the waves. The others didn't notice his leaving. Only one old man on the shore stood to watch.

Long after Laika's figure had disappeared into the mists of distance, a speck of gold remained in the sky, now and then returning a blinding flash of light.

"We will listen to these hymns . . ." the old man said.

The Poet in His Labyrinth
BY SILAS HASLAM
(TRANSLATED BY JOSEPH MARTIN)

He had dreamed of a verse, and when he woke, he found he had dragged it back with him across the viscous borderland of sleep. *We will listen to these hymns and attach wings of gold to them, and they will cross the sea.* He repeated it out loud, listening along with the words. *We will listen to these hymns and attach wings of gold to them, and they will cross the sea.* The images were familiar, but the words themselves were a mystery until he realized that someone—something?—had translated them into English. And as he thought this, another thought simultaneously told him that both these thoughts and the earlier one had also been translated. He ordered himself to think in Spanish, but the order itself was delivered in English.

He understood then that he had woken on the other side of something, a place that he had no name for. He stood. It was dark. At first he thought he was outside, in the fields. But when he looked to the heavens, he saw they were black except for points of candlelight, evenly spaced. He was indoors, but this was an indoors he had never seen and could not describe in words. He began to walk. Again, he grasped for the rounded vessel of his native tongue, and again the words that returned to him were his, but not his own. *That I am a dead man, still walking, is clear.* His limbs felt light and insubstantial, but they cast small shadows in the strange, steady candlelight. With each step, he felt the life flowing out of him. He was still in some borderland and must find his way home. The place was quiet, empty of men. He had woken near a bank of chairs, and he walked toward them now, slowly, taking care because of his legs. From a distance the chairs seemed to be floating, but when he came close, he saw that they were merely connected one to another, the whole series resting on a single shiny base. What miracles man was capable of! *Everything could be invented except wings.* He passed through a corridor and came to a crossroads. He hesitated for a moment before turning left and following another corridor. Here the sky was lower, though still studded with faint candlelight. Shiny paintings lined the walls. At first, he mistook them for windows. The poet moved closer to inspect them. He recognized the sea and recoiled, understanding that he was back, somehow, in his native land. How his compatriots loved the sea, the huge flat level sea. *My aim is the sky,* he thought, though these were not the words he would have chosen. It was early winter—that much he could tell—and the air was pleasant. At the end of the corridor he came to another crossroads and turned left, this time without hesitation. Here the space opened up on both sides of the corridor. Banks and banks of the slender chairs were lined up in rows on either side of him. Beyond the chairs loomed the largest windows he had ever seen, and beyond them, the night. So this was it: he had woken in some kind of purgatory, a great waiting room in some train station he could not describe. The poet's footsteps resounded on the bare floor, though he objected to this construction as well, especially to the word "resounded." Above him, numbers flashed in red lights. Perhaps these were related to Edison's invention. But the poet could not decipher them: 06:21. He stood under the light and after a moment, the display changed again: 06:22. The poet stood and counted. At 06:23, he understood that this was a new kind of precise and unforgiving clock, its malignant silence marking time with neither pity nor poetry.

He walked on. The darkened glass was further obscured by condensation, as if he were moving inside a bubble of artificial air. Such things were possible, he knew. He was an educated man, had read in his time Verne and Whitman, had found in Verne a kinsman. As for the American, Whitman was not always in the best of taste, but audacious, alive, unencumbered: a winged angel. Such things were possible only for Americans. His own countrymen would always be weighted with history, constrained by the straitjacket he himself had woven. The poet knew this without having to tell it to himself. But if only he could think without words. He was weary of the foreign tongue in his mind, as weary as he had grown of so many of the things of this world before falling asleep and waking here in this lonely limbo.

At the end of the long, wide corridor, the poet found himself at another crossroads and turned left. Now he had to find a way out. Here there was no place to rest. No one to hear him shout. No point to this endless quest. Another bank of chairs and, in one of them, a book. He hoped it was a book of poetry. He picked it up to find it as light and insubstantial as his legs. *Loving Che*, left behind by a tourist who would not miss it. A novel, by the look of it. The genre did not please him. *There is so much feigning in a novel and the joys of artistic creation do not make up for the pain of moving through that prolonged fiction, surrounded by dialogues that have never been heard between people who have never lived.* He returned the book to the chair and continued looking for an exit. What devil had landed him here? What malevolent spirit was filling his mind with foreign words?

All these years without speech and to find himself now, unable to effect the simplest of ideas or to form one last thought in his native tongue. He reached the final corridor, turned left, and stopped before a scene so baffling that he lost all ability to express it, even to himself. Overhead in gold letters was his own name written beside indecipherable symbols. Beyond them, dawn had lit an impossible place: an imagined universe populated by cylindrical train cars, each of them winged, waiting like giant birds atop their wheeled legs. The poet stood, in awe, before coming slowly to his knees. He kissed the ground before such mysteries. Truly, he was a minor thing in this world.

Already he understood the symbol, knew his time had come. Behind him, the flurry of footsteps and men shouting in that other language that he could no longer form to his liking. Though he could not comprehend, still the rhythm was beautiful and he was overcome by nostalgia: an ancient memory of his mother, the soft syllables of her good-bye. The poet stood and waited for the handcuffs, the familiar rhythm of imprisonment and death. He tried one last time to say what he meant, but failed. The men who led him away handled him roughly. The poet returned to them a smile: "Gentlemen," he said, "there are affections of such delicate honesty . . ."

Adios Happy Homeland:

Selected Translations According to Google

We had wanted a machine that could translate; we got a machine that transforms stories.
—Ricardo Piglia, *The Absent City*

The Breaking

by Gertrudis Gómez de Avellaneda y Arteaga

Pearl of the sea! Star of the West!
Beautiful Cuba! Your bright sky
The night her gloomy veil covered with
As it covers the pain my sad face.

I'll go! . . . The mob diligent
To tear me from the land
The hoist sail, and soon his vigilance
The breeze comes your burning zone.

Adios happy homeland, dear Eden!
Where'er the wrath of fate impels me.
Your sweet name flatter my ear!

Adios! . . . I turgid rustling sail . . .
The anchor stands . . . the ship
Shaken,
The short waves and silent fly!

Simple Lines (fragments)
by José Martí

I am an honest man
From where the palm grows,
And before I die
Browse verses from my soul.

I come from everywhere to everywhere
And: I am art among the arts,
in the mountains I am.

I know the strange names of the herbs and flowers,
Fatal deception, and sublime pain.

I have seen in the night softly fall on my head
pure light rays of the divine beauty.

Alas vi born on the shoulders of beautiful women
and out of the rubble, flying butterflies.

I've seen live in a man with the dagger at his side,
And never the name of those who killed him.

Quick, like a reflection, Twice I saw the soul, two:
When my poor father died, when she bade me farewell.

*I shivered once—at the gate, at the entrance to the
    vineyard,—
When the barbarian bee stung on the forehead to my
    child.*

*I enjoyed it once, so that you never enjoyed—
when the sentence of death read the mayor crying.*

*I hear a sigh, through land and sea, and not a sigh,
—is that my son will wake up.*

*If they say that the jeweler Take trove,
a sincere friend and I put aside love.*

*I have seen the wounded eagle fly the blue serene,
And die in his lair The snake's venom.*

*I know that when the world Cede, livid, to rest on the
    profound silence
murmurs gentle stream.*

*I have placed a bold hand, rigid with horror and joy,
On the star that fell dead in front of my door.*

*Hidden in my brave heart punishment that hurts me:
The son of an enslaved people live for it, suffers and dies.*

Everything is beautiful,
All is music and reason,
And all, like diamond,
is carbon before it is light.

I know that the fool is buried with great luxury and tears.
And no fruit on earth Like the cemetery.

Callo, and understand,
and I take the pomp of rhyming:
hang a withered tree in my hood doctor.

The Shadow of My Memories
by Ursula de Céspedes y Orellano

. . . Listen: all my hours
slip into silence
lulled by the sad
monotony of my prayers

There is no smile on my lips
and in my eyes and no fire;
but those are no complaints
and they always tears.

My forehead lies folded
under the formidable weight

of infinite bitterness
and an immense misfortune. . . .

But where is it? There is no longer
has vanished
like those light clouds
that evaporate in the wind;

With that she left me
without hearing my accent? . . .
Indeed it was so sad
what he was saying.

Who is she did not
to last a long time?
The chimera of the past
the shadow of my memories.

Mockingbird and Tocoloro

by José Jacinto Milanés y Fuentes

Among the birds of the mountain
hot idol worship,
brighter than the tocoloro,
the mockingbird sings better.

Two hunters will adore
Canasí pretty flower,
hope your other two
And waiting penamos.
While we do not enjoy themselves
that lift us up to heaven,
to listen, my love, get ready
I conceived the idea
my opponent and me
among birds of the forest

One afternoon in my roan,
mimics my sadness,
I walked through a grove,
perdióseme where the trail.
In a high caimitillo
I saw a choir singing
a mockingbird, a tocoloro—
and my rival brooding,
and so I cried,
hot idol worship.

Although grace on me
and although I have no bad peak
he is rich tocoloro
Mockingbird and I am poor.

Who is that patience copper
dead love, and no gold?
Who does not melt into mourning
seeing, holding,
although not sing
brighter than the tocoloro?

But I hope, pretty flower,
Canasí pretty flower,
your looking at my
not money but love.
My hope is not error,
and although the tocoloro apronte
his pen, which adds to the mountain
will have their song by husky
as always and everywhere trunk
the mockingbird sings better.

Del Alférez Machicao Cristóbal de la Coba, Ruler of This Villa

by Silvestre de Balboa Troya y Quesada

So high you fly, bird Canario
that we lose sight and your flight
flow like an eagle rising to heaven
to seek his remedy in his hand.

You with extra-ordinary new style
your fame extends the wide ground
counting the prison and grief
Holy Vicar of the Divine Shepherd.

Baja high tower of Elicona
where your course is up wit you
to this fragile our hands.

And gird your brow the Crown
by Laurel beautiful without seasoning caught
Get your mother Gran Canaria

Twilight
by Juana Borrero

Everything is quiet and peace . . . In the shadows
breathe the scent of jasmine,
and, beyond, on the glass of river
heard the flapping of swans

that as a group of snow flowers
slide down the smooth surface.
The dark bats reappear
its thousand hidden locations

and around a thousand, and whimsical drawings
described by the tranquil atmosphere;
or fly then tracking the soil,

barely touching his gray wings
of sour milk thistle yellow petal
corolla mauve humble virgin.

Nostalgias
by José Julián Herculano del Casal y de la Lastra

1
Sigh regions
where kingfishers fly
on the sea
and the icy breath of wind
appears in their movement
sob;

where the snow coming down
the sky, shrouded
the green
fragrant fields
and rivers
the rumor;

which always holds the sky
air through the veil,
gray;
the moon is more beautiful
and each star a
lily.

The North Station
by José María Heredia y Heredia

Temples and the tedious summer
The fire burning: the stiff pole
Of the north winds shaken,
Are wrapped in fog dark
And get rid of fever Cuba impure.

Ruge deep sea, swollen breast
And whipping strikes hit the beaches:
Their wings bathed in fresh Zephyr,
And gauzy, transparent veil
Surrounds the Sun and the shining sky.

Health, happy days! A death
The bloody altar that May derribáis
Between rose flowers: the accompanying
With yellow fever face unholy
And with a melancholy radiance glowed.

Both were with stern face
In the temperate zones to children
Under the burning sky and burning:
With his pale scepters they touched,
And the fatal tumble down the pit.

But his empire fine: the north wind,
Poisoned air purifying,
Spreads its wings wet and cold
For our fields resonating flies
And the strictness of the consoles in August.

Today in the climates of Europe sad
Enraged blow from the north
His life and removes green fields,
Snow covers the bare ground,
And the man holds stiff in his mansion.

Everything is death and pain, however in Cuba
Everything is life and pleasure: Phoebus smiles
But the clouds tempered transparent
Gives new luster to the forest and prairie,
And the animals in a double spring.

Homeland happy! You, favored
Pleased with the look and smile
Of God! Not your fields

I snatch back the fiery fate.
Lúzcame ay! the sun in your sky last.

Oh! With much pleasure, my love
About the humble roof that covers us
Hear the quiet falling rain
And we heard the whistling wind,
And the distant ocean the roaring!

Fill my glass with golden wine
That scares care and pain:
He adored my hungry mouth
Very pleased to be with you further tested
And sweetest lips touched.

Together with you lying in spring seat
On your knees pulsars my lyre,
And sing happy my love, my homeland,
In your face and your soul's beauty,
And your love unspeakable and my happiness.

A Found Poem
by Alejo Carpentier

I wondered sometimes
if the highest forms of aesthetic
emotion does not consist simply
of a supreme understanding of creation.

One day, the men find an alphabet
in the eyes of the chalcedony,
the brown velvet of the moth,
and then astonished to know
each snail was spotted, always,
a poem.

Un Cuento Extraño
by Nitza Pol-Villa

"Tradúceme esto," dijo Phillip.

Michael tomó los papeles y les dio una ojeada antes de devolvérselos a su amigo.

"No conozco este idioma."

"¿Como que no conoces el idioma?"

"Que no lo conozco, *man*," dijo Michael.

Phillip tomó los papeles en sus manos. Los contempló con una gran tristeza, una tristeza muy anciana, una tristeza que se deslizaba por los senderos de esta extraña ciudad y alcanzaba, tras vínculos dolorosos y destrozados, hasta la fuente: las grandes avenidas y floreadas vistas de su tierra lejana, Bergen County, New Jersey.

Las vicisitudes de la vida lo habían traído aquí, a este puerto desteñido en un olvidado rincón del Caribe. Phillip y Michael se habían conocido una tarde resplendente de sol y su amistad consistía, como muchas parecidas, en su mutua historia. No eran amigos cercanos, pero sí de esa manera tan común en el exilio que supone que las personas que provienen del mismo lugar ya se conocen en el fondo de sus almas. Esto es ilusión, por cierto. Pero una ilusión deliciosa cuando uno se encuentra en países lejanos.

"Bueno, *buddy*," dijo Phillip al fin, "si dices que no conoces el idioma, pues, qué se va hacer." Y con eso, Phillip dobló los papeles y los devolvió a su mochila.

Si Michael sintió alguna curiosidad sobre el contenido de los papeles, no lo dejo saber. Pero Phillip estaba seguro de que antes de que callera la tarde, Michael le preguntaría por ellos. Entonces Phillip se lo contaría todo.

Los amigos estaban sentados al aire libre en una cafetería favorita a unos pasos del Malecón. Era invierno y el aire tenía un dulzor que hizo los hombres recordar las primaveras de su niñez. Ordenaron unas cervezas y Phillip desenrolló su *home-made grid* y los dos saquitos de monedas que utilizaban para el *Go!* Phillip había aprendido a jugarlo durante su servicio en Vietnam—o es mejor decir, durante su convalecencia—y cuando conoció a Michael, lo primero que hizo fue enseñarle los rudimentos del juego.

Ordenaron dos cervezas más y unos sándwiches—dicen que el último refugio del recuerdo es la comida, y los dos amigos todavía no se habían acomodado al paladar caribeño. Masticaban y jugaban en silencio. Parecían dos turistas alemanes—de los cuales se daban mucho en este país—rosaditos y gorditos: Phillip en camisa de mangas cortas y Michael en uno de sus *polo shirt*. Después de un rato, las monedas de Phillip habían conquistado la pista.

"*Shit!*" dijo Michael. Odiaba perder.

"Tu problema es que sigues comportándote como si fuera esto un juego de chance," dijo Phillip. La verdad era que su amigo jugaba como un muerto. Las monedas llegaban al *grid* sin vida. *Go!* no era un juego cualquiera; no era suficiente dejarse llevar por las corrientes. A Phillip le tomó años entender la sutilezas de ese mundo que sólo aparentaba existir en blanco y negro. Quizás, para entender bien, uno tendría que haber sufrido un poco, tendría que conocer la estrategia de engaño que se necesita para sobrevivir y, más que nada, tenía que aceptar que una mal jugada al inicio, podría tener repercusiones en el futuro lejano. El tiempo existía como una serie de puntos que conectan. Pero como explicarle ese sentido a alguien como Michael.

Phillip había sido paracaidista, miembro de la Tercera Brigada del 505, y nunca olvido la sensación de estar suspendido sobre la tierra. Muchas veces sintió que el mundo mismo se recogía hacia él. Y aún hoy, tantos años después de su última y desastrosa misión, a veces despertaba con la certidumbre de que el futuro avanzaba hacia él mientras él quedaba suspendido en un presente perpetuo.

Pidieron dos cafés americanos. Phillip propuso un juego más, pero Michael se negó. Tomo su café en silencio. Así habían pasado muchos días desde su exilio—sentados en ese café mosqueado, tomando cervezas y café, contemplando la vida que pasaba entre sus manos como si tuvieran todo el tiempo del mundo. Después de un rato, Michael habló.

"¿Y de que se tratan los papeles?"

Phillip sonrío. "¿Cuáles papeles?"

Michael lo miró fijamente. "No seas un *jerk*."

"*Oh*, los papeles que necesitan traducción," respondió Phillip. "*Oh well*, no tienen importancia ahora."

Michael hizo un gesto, como si intentara decir algo. Pero mantuvo su silencio.

Caía la tarde. Se destapó una brisa fragante. La juventud ya se acercaba al Malecón. Cuando paso una chica bonita por la mesa, Phillip no pudo resistir un piropo—era de otra época y no sabía que estas cosas habían pasado de moda, aun en el Caribe.

"*Mother of God!*" dijo, "*I hope you know CPR, 'cause you take my breath away.*"

La muchacha no le prestó atención.

"Viejo verde," dijo Michael, rompiendo el silencio.

"*Don't fuck with me*," dijo Phillip. "Eres tan viejo como yo."

"Pero no tan verde."

"Quizás rosado."

Michael lo ignoró. Después de un rato, dijo, "¿Y que querrá decir eso?"

"¿Decir qué?" dijo Phillip, todavía un poco dolido por el rechazo de la muchacha (en su mente seguía siendo un joven guapo) y también por las palabras de su amigo.

"Viejo verde."

"¡Otra vez con eso!"

"¿No, viejo, que de dónde vendrá esa frase?"

"¿Cuál?"

"Viejo verde."

"Pues, no te entiendo," dijo Phillip.

"*Green old man*," dijo Michael. "Tampoco lo entiendo yo."

"Ah, ya entiendo lo que quieres decir. Pues 'viejo verde' es solamente una manera de hablar," dijo Phillip. "No hay que entenderlo todo."

"Quizás tengas razón," dijo Michael. "Pero confieso que no entiendo la gran parte de lo que hablo yo mismo."

"Ni yo," dijo Phillip, *grateful at last to acknowledge something that had long bothered him*. "¿Por ejemplo, por qué hablamos en castellano, cuando la lengua de ambos es el inglés?"

"Precisamente," dijo Michael. "He estado contemplando ese *riddle* hace tiempo ya."

"No tiene sentido."

"No, es cierto, para nosotros no tiene sentido. Pero quizás para alguien sí."

"¿Para quién?"

"No sé. Para la que escribe el cuento, quizás. Sabes bien que se desarrolla en el Caribe, y en el Caribe se habla español."

"Que comemierda eres. En el Caribe también se habla inglés y francés."

"Tienes razón. ¿Entonces no se por qué carajo nos tiene hablando español?"

Los dos callaron. Después de un rato, llegó la camarera. "Desean algo más," preguntó la chica.

"¿Pues, nos puedes explicar por qué dos norteamericanos están hablando castellano entre ellos?" dijo Michael.

"Algo más de tomar quiero decir," dijo la muchacha.

"No estás para la filosofía hoy," dijo Michael.

La camarera recogió los vasos de la mesa. "Ni hoy, ni nunca," dijo. "Hay que trabajar, no pensar."

"Bien," dijo Phillip. "Sólo la cuenta."

La muchacha afirmo silenciosamente y se fue.

"La cuenta, . . ." repitió Michael, como en un sueño. "La cuenta será la esposa del cuento?"

"Sólo de los cuentos extraños," respondió Phillip.

"You have reason," dijo Michael.

"Ya lo ves," dijo Phillip. "Lo transporto en esta mochila."

"La."

"¿La, que?"

"La razón," dijo Michael. "En español es femenina."

"Y en inglés no es . . . nada," dijo Phillip, como asombrado.

"*Strange*," dijo Michael.

See anamenendezonline.com for an English language translation of this story.

A Brief History of the Cuban Poets
BY VICTORIA O'CAMPO

There once was a country of dark wounds, known for exiling and murdering its poets. This was a sad and often bloody tradition that, like most of its kind, dated back to the Spanish. The first of these tragic poets was born in Santiago de Cuba in 1803. In 1823, he was arrested and charged with conspiring against the oppressors. He was forced to flee to Mexico, where he died, too young, in 1839.

In 1812, another poet was born, in San Diego de Núñez. When he was not yet thirty, he began to participate in the struggle against the oppressors. In 1848 the poet was arrested, but he managed to escape to New York City, where he died on October 24, 1894, never to see his country free. There was also a woman who was born in Puerto Príncipe in 1814. When she was nine, her father died and her mother remarried a Spanish officer. At twenty-two, she was forced to leave Cuba with her new family for La Coruña. She took many lovers, and they all died. She had a child out of wedlock with a poet, who left her when the child was born, claiming it wasn't his. The child also died. She married another poet, and he died. Devastated, she entered a convent, where she wrote a play that got terrible reviews.[9]

---

9.   **Al Partir**
¡Perla del mar! ¡Estrella de Occidente!

The doomed poet of Bayamo was born in 1818. In the 1860s he took part in an uprising against the oppressors and was captured; he was executed on a particularly windy day in August 1870.

The most famous of this unlucky lot was born in 1853 in Havana. Like the doomed poet of Bayamo, this doomed poet of Havana took part in the uprising of the 1860s against the oppressors. At sixteen, he was arrested and imprisoned. His parents could do nothing to free him. His legs bled where the chains chafed him. He became so ill that the oppressors exiled him to Spain. But he could not remain in one place—the particular curse of the island poets. He lived in Spain, Mexico, and Guatemala before sneaking back into Cuba and then fleeing once more to New York. In 1893, he traveled through Central America, the West Indies, and Florida, raising money and enthusiasm for the

---

¡Hermosa Cuba! Tu brillante cielo
La noche cubre con su opaco velo,
Como cubre el dolor mi triste frente.

¡Voy á partir! . . . La chusma diligente
Para arrancarme del nativo suelo
Las velas iza, y pronta á su desvelo
La brisa acude de tu zona ardiente.

¡Adiós, patria feliz, Edén querido!
Doquier que el hado en su furor me impela,
Tu dulce nombre halagará mi oído!

¡Adiós! . . . ¡ya cruje la turgente vela . . .
El ancla se alza . . . el buque estremecido
Las olas corta y silenciosa vuela!

fight against the oppressors. In 1895, he returned to the island for the last time. On May 19, he led a charge against the oppressors at the Battle of Two Rivers and was killed.

A silver-tongued poet was born in Havana in 1871. At thirteen, he fled the oppressors with his family to Key West. He returned as an adult and tried to join public life but again had to resign because of the oppressors.

In 1892, another unsuspecting poet was born in Camagüey. He went to Spain to fight the oppressors, and when that didn't work out, fled to Mexico, where he collaborated with the next round of oppressors.

A few years later, in 1899, a woman poet was born. She was exiled by the oppressors in 1960 and died in Miami in 1991, the lucky beneficiary of a long life not usually granted to poets of that island.

We come now to the granddaughter of a great national hero. She was born in Rome in 1911, but could not escape the curse of the island poets. In 1935, she was jailed for agitating against the oppressors.

In 1912, a poet was born who would be exiled by one oppressor for his politics and isolated by another for his tendencies. He died in 1979, unrecognized and alone.

In 1930, in Oriente, a poet was born who would be forced to flee the oppressors in 1945.

Another poet was born to a poor family in 1931. He fought two different oppressors, was jailed, and died in a hunger strike in prison in 1972.

The poet of audacious roses was born in 1932 in Puerta de Golpe. At first he was a supporter of the oppressors, but by the late 1960s he was criticizing them. The oppressors put him under house arrest after he published a book they didn't like. They asked him a lot of questions, and when the poet of audacious roses had to appear before his peers and confess his crimes, international intellectuals were appalled. But the oppressors were undeterred and kept up the harassment for almost a decade. In 1980, he was finally exiled to the United States, where he died in 2000.

Is this sounding like a broken record? In 1945, a poet was born in Morón. At first, he, too, supported the oppressors. But in 1989, he signed a petition for the release of political prisoners. Things went downhill for him. In 2003, the oppressors rounded him up along with several other writers and thinkers. He was convicted of insufficient zeal and sentenced to twenty years in jail. After a year in a windowless cell, he was exiled to Spain.

In 1959 another poet was born in Havana. She grew up to become an anarchist who fought the oppressors with words and vandalism. In 1978, she was sentenced to twenty years in prison. But in 1980, the government mistakenly released her from Paradise and sent her to Florida.

We end with the poet who was born in the poor country-side of Oriente in 1943. Like others before him, he was initially enamored of the oppressors. But this admiration soon wore off after he was harassed and imprisoned for various offenses against the empire of reason, including, but not limited to, a proclivity for writing poems on the leaves of innocent trees. In 1980, he managed to escape across the Straits in disguise. In 1990, in New York City, he took his life, still dreaming of returning to the sea.

The Melancholy Hour
by Gertrudis Gómez

The hotel looked out over the old church, and on their first afternoon in the city, the woman and the poet stood behind the translucent curtains and watched the tourists move like shadows in the lighted square below.

They had been meeting here for many years and always came away thinking that the days had been too short. They never fought, but for the first time they had carried to their meeting the burden of a misunderstanding. It was the usual sort of misunderstanding that passes between men and women, but like all the others they thought theirs unique and especially regrettable.

As most of their correspondence on the matter took place through letters, their conversation became imbued with all the worst aspects of writing—metaphors, allusions, foreshadowings, tricks of perspective—that served only to deepen the crisis. They each passed several bad nights before agreeing to put off any more discussion until they met again.

Once they arrived at the hotel with the pleasant staff and the painted cherubs on the wall, and were again secure in each other's presence, the worst of the misunderstanding seemed to fall away. In this way, they passed several pleasant days. The woman, especially, was relieved, for she was beginning to feel that familiar

ANA MENÉNDEZ

sliding away, the desire—that always struck at twilight—to pull down the curtains on the world and fly.

Their last night in the city, the man and the woman dined at a restaurant around the block. A man sang in a language neither recognized. After the meal, they walked back to their hotel slowly. It was a fine summer night and the breeze was good. They passed the old church, and then its long, lonely yard. The woman shivered. At the entrance they heard a faint calling and came closer. A young voice chanted, "*Es la hora melancólica, indecisa, en que pueblan los sueños los espacios, y en los aires—con soplos de la brisa—levantan sus fantásticos palacios.*"

The man pulled the woman away, but she had time to hear the voice, high with laughter, repeat, "*Y en los aires—con soplos de la brisa—levantan sus fantásticos palacios.*"

They stopped in front of the hotel. A sound like the fluttering of birds' wings made them look up.

Through the translucent curtains, the wind blew hard. Up above, in the room that was theirs, two shadows moved against the light. The woman and the poet watched for a long time, night falling.

At last the woman spoke. "Shall we go and tell them?"

"No," said the man. "Let them linger there a little while longer."

End-less Stories
BY ANONYMOUS

The Story of the Good Pipe

This is a true story told to me when I was a little girl growing up in Tampa, Florida. It's a very old children's story told throughout the Spanish-speaking world. The first time you hear it, you are very excited, because you are about to hear a story you've never heard before. The second time you hear it, you run out of the room, screaming.

So do you want me to tell you the story of the good pipe? If *Yes*, go to 1. If *No*, go to 2.

1. Now, let's see. I didn't say, "Yes." I said, "Do you want me to tell you the story of the good pipe?" So, do you want to hear the story of the good pipe? If *Yes*, go to 3. If *No*, go to 4.

2. Come on, I didn't say, "No." You very clearly heard me say, "Do you want me to tell you the story of the good pipe?" So, do you want to hear the story of the good pipe? If *Yes*, go to 1. If *No*, go to 4.

3. How many times do I have to tell you? I didn't say, "Yes." I said, "Do you want me to tell you the story of the good pipe?" So, do you want to hear it or not? If *Yes*, go to 1. If *No*, go to 2.

4. How many times do I have to tell you? I didn't say, "No." I said, "Do you want me to tell you the story of the good pipe?" So, do you want to hear it or not? If *Yes*, go to 1. If *No*, go to 2.

The Locust and the Mockingbird

Once upon a time in Cuba, there lived a sugar king with a very beautiful daughter. Princes came from all over the country and beyond, wishing to marry her. But the king didn't think anyone would ever be good enough for his daughter, so he said that he would consent to her marriage on one condition only. If a man could be found with the ability to tell an endless story, he would have the daughter's hand. But beware to those who failed: they would be beheaded. So many princes came and tried to tell an endless story, but they could not. Each was beheaded. Finally, after a year of this mad carnage, a poor country boy appeared at court. "Sir," he said, "I have come to tell an endless story." The bloodthirsty king took one look at the ruffian and smiled. What the king didn't know was that the lad had been trained in BASIC programming. "Please, begin," the king said. So the boy did. To begin reading the boy's story, go to 1. If you prefer not to hear it, go to 2.

1. In my town, east of Oriente, there once lived a man who was mad for corn. He bought the grain from all ends of the earth and eventually he had to build a barn to house it. If you want to continue to read the story, go to 3. Otherwise, go to 2.

2. Go to 1.

3. The barn covered an entire acre and was several stories high. When it was done, the man filled it to the ceiling with his corn. But the man was not as expert a carpenter as he believed himself to be, and he left a tiny hole at the very top where the roof beams joined. To continue reading the story, go to 4. Otherwise, go to 2.

4. The hole in the barn roof was large enough for a single grain of corn to pass through. Soon enough, along came a locust, and he squeezed through the hole and took a grain of corn. He flew with his single grain of corn to his home and dropped it off, and then flew back to the barn to fetch another. To continue reading, go to 5. Otherwise, go to 2.

5. While the locust was gone, a little mockingbird who was kindly disposed to the farmer spied the corn and flew back to the barn, where the locust was just leaving with another grain of corn. As the locust flew away, the little bird let the grain of corn he was carrying in his beak drop back in through the hole in the barn. To continue reading, go to 6. If you wish to stop reading right now, go to 2. If you think it implausible that a mockingbird should be kindly disposed toward a farmer, go to 7.

6. The locust returned to his home, dropped off his grain of corn, and flew back to the barn to fetch another. To continue reading, go to 5. Otherwise, go to 2.

7. Nevertheless, it is true, as I saw it with my own eyes. To continue reading, go to 6. Otherwise, go to 2.

The Can of Infinite Stories

1. One day, a boy was walking in the swamp when he came upon a dusty can. As it was quite heavy, the boy thought it might contain a good meal. Thinking how pleased his mother would be, the boy immediately set about polishing the can. But no sooner had he shined the surface to a mirror finish than a foreign melody began to play and smoke seeped out through the joints. In fear, the boy threw the thing down. As soon as the can hit the ground, however, the lid popped open and out jumped a man dressed in a sparkling embroidered gown. Speaking in a strange accent from a movie the boy had forgotten, the man said: "Because you have freed me from this can of Goya Black Beans, I will now tell you a story without end." If you think the boy consented to hear the story, go to 2. Otherwise, go to 3.

2. "Excellent!" the boy said. In truth, he had grown weary of the usual stories with their tidy endings and stock characters and he longed for something different. Seeing this, the tin-can man was very pleased, and he began to tell a story. To read the story the man from the can of Goya Black Beans told the boy, go to 1. Otherwise, go to 4.

3. You're wrong. Go to 2.

4. It's too late to back out now, unfortunately. Go to 1.

Three Betrayals
BY JANE SMITH

There are affections of such delicate honesty that they can be re-kindled after decades of silence. I have known Gertrudis Gómez since childhood. We went to elementary school together and then middle school and then high school, where we both gradu-ated at the top of our class. She already knew she wanted to be a journalist and I already knew I would be an attorney—cor-porate law, though later I changed my mind and took up family law. After graduation we went to different universities—she to Columbia and I to Harvard—and we lost touch, as happens.

For almost ten years I worked for a big New York firm, where I experienced the usual things: boredom, ennui, the com-bination of helplessness and terror that in our age we refer to as "stress." In 2004, I moved back to Miami to open my own practice. Times were good, economically, which means that they were good for me as well. Boom times, I'm sorry to say, favor divorce. I was maybe six months into my move when I received a call from Gertrudis, who wanted to file for divorce and asked if she could come by to talk.

Some fifteen years had passed since I'd last seen her, but Gertrudis seemed little changed. I recognized her right away and also noted her slight hesitation on seeing me. I was acutely aware, then, of having changed quite a bit. I had put on weight since high school, and the years at the firm had not been good to my complexion or my health. But if I felt at a slight disadvantage, Gertrudis did everything to quickly dispel the feeling. She was as positive and energetic as a teenage girl, and as lovely. But beneath this polished (surgically enhanced?) exterior there also moved a mature calm, a grace calculated to put people at ease. I suppose it was an occupational trick—a different kind of which had made me a fairly blunt creature. But there was in it also the affection of adolescence; the many years of shared triumphs and hopes. I agreed to take the case, and Gertrudis filled me in on her life since 1988. She had, as promised, become a journalist. After receiving her MS from Columbia, she had gone straight to work for the *Wall Street Journal*, where she had quickly risen. She was good at what she did. She had learned, she told me, that the way to get people to talk was to be kind and accommodating. Rudeness worked only in the Hollywood version, and, at any rate, should be considered a last resort. "You have to make people feel comfortable," she said, "if you want them to tell you anything." She had met her husband on the job, at some industry thing she was covering. Mathieu Boreas worked in investment banking. I later learned that his specialty had been the CDOs that brought down the U.S. economy in 2007. But a nice guy, by the look of it. Handsome, wealthy, with an apartment in Paris. They traveled a lot during the first years of the marriage. When the paper transferred Gertrudis to Hong Kong, Mathieu arranged to work out of his firm's office there. From Hong

Kong it was on to Brussels, followed by a stint in London, this time dictated by her husband's work, and finally a move back to Miami, where for the past two years Gertrudis had been covering Latin American business and Mathieu had overseen the opening of a new branch.

"Exciting life," I said.

"Yes," she said, and there was nothing bitter in her voice, only a kind of wonder.

They'd never had children, Gertrudis said. To which I replied, without thinking, "Good, that will make things easier." A small cloud seemed to pass over her. I explained myself, adding that I had seen many friendly divorces, none of them with children.

"The presence of children," I said, "makes people crazy."

"A lot more is at stake," Gertrudis said, in a tone that made it impossible to gauge the depths of whatever it was I had stirred.

Four years ago, the marriage had started to unravel. *Unravel* —I don't know why we so often use that verb to describe a marriage in trouble. *Unravel, come apart, disentangle.* I suppose marriage is a sort of protective layer woven by two people, and it takes some time to unweave. Who had pulled the first string? By the sound of it, that had been her husband. The both of them traveled a lot, and as any divorce attorney can tell you, this is the kiss of death for a marriage. But like most, Gertrudis and Mathieu Boreas thought they would be the ones to beat the odds.

"A few years ago, his trips became different," Gertrudis said.

"In what way?"

"Hard to say." She thought for a moment. "Indefinite. He couldn't say when he was leaving or when he was coming back, exactly. Sometimes, he'd be due back on a Tuesday and he would call to say he was delayed until after the weekend. That kind of thing."

He started missing birthdays and holidays. He grew "distant" and surly. Then he stopped sleeping with her.

It's always a bit awkward the first time a client offers personal details of her sex life, but you get used to it. There's a lot to the saying that marriages fail because of either money or sex. And in both cases, the aggrieved party wants you, the attorney, to know it. People need to communicate their suffering, a human quirk that Gertrudis must have also been intimately acquainted with. At any rate, Gertrudis seemed to have taken the withdrawal of intimacy hardest. When she discovered he'd been surfing porn on the home computer, she lost it.

"You won't sleep with me, but you watch this trash," she said she had told him. She told me this in a calm voice, which contrasted with the scene as it must have actually played out. But Mathieu had denied it to the end.

"Why, when I have such a beautiful wife, would I do such a thing?" he asked. And she had let the matter drop, unresolved.

Six months ago, Mathieu had missed Christmas for the second year in a row. He'd had to fly to London at the last minute. "Urgent meeting with the European team," he said. He returned from the trip on December 28 more distant and angry than usual.

"He was pissed off about something, pissed off at me, but I couldn't for the life of me figure it out," Gertrudis said. "It felt so unfair."

They lived in a spacious duplex apartment on Brickell Key. Gertrudis noticed that Mathieu was unusually protective of his briefcase on the afternoon of his return. He kept it by his side as they talked in the living room and then took it with him to the office before even going to the bathroom to wash up after his travels. Gertrudis checked on him in his office later that evening and found him at the computer. The briefcase was on a chair, and before she could pick it up, Mathieu stood quickly and took it from her reach.

"I've been a journalist for fifteen years," Gertrudis told me. "I notice things."

So that night, as her husband slept beside her, Gertrudis rose and went looking for the briefcase. It took her a while, but she found it where he had stuffed it in an empty filing cabinet.

"I opened the case and it was the first thing I pulled out," she told me. "Two first-class tickets to Costa Rica, departing December 21, returning December 28. In the names of Mathieu Boreas and Samantha Trastavere."

I knew well enough to say nothing, only nod. She could continue or not, as she wished. "This Samantha," she said, "was a woman I had heard of many times before, of course. How funny she was, how the young traders were all in love with her. I may have even met her once at one of the insufferable parties they put on."

"Do you have copies of the tickets?"

Gertrudis smiled. "I have the tickets themselves," she said. "I slipped them into a hardcover in the library." She paused and added, with a smile: "Bertrand Russell."

She brought the tickets to the next meeting and I had my secretary photocopy them. Florida is a no-fault state, which means a fifty-fifty split of the assets, no matter what. However, if you can prove that there has been a squandering of the marital wealth, say with a lover, the aggrieved party can recover her share. I explained this to Gertrudis, who listened without nodding or disagreeing—displaying a complete lack of emotion that unnerved me. I told her we would subpoena the girlfriend, take some depos, and hire a forensic accountant to go through the books. This last was absolutely crucial, I told her, given her husband's profession. Gertrudis let me talk, and when I was finished she said simply, "No."

Then she told me the rest of the story. About four years back, she had gone to cover a conference in Cartagena and had met a poet, a Cuban man, now living in Venezuela. They became lovers. So far, none of this really surprised me. Typical stuff. What was unusual was Gertrudis's complete lack of self-justification. At this point in the narrative, most clients will tell you how this person made them feel alive, how they rediscovered their passion for life, how they understood that they had been living a corrosive lie until then, etc. Gertrudis spared me all this—she was too smart or too discreet to offer excuses or explanations. Similarly, she avoided tears of guilt or self-recrimination. Her only allowance to sentiment was an inscrutable (at least to me) comment about what had attracted her to this man. "He let me touch his face," she said.

Theirs became an international affair. She was living in London at the time, and he was dividing his time between Venezuela, where he had a family, and Paris, where he had initially been granted asylum. When he was in Europe, she traveled to meet him, always coordinating her assignations with her work. This went on for years, Gertrudis told me, and she didn't tell me anything to suggest when—or if—the relationship had ended. This poet was the first person she had told about the tickets to Costa Rica, and he had advised her, in his calm way, not to make any hasty decisions that she would later regret. She understood immediately what he meant, of course. "It's one thing for two married adults to carry on a long affair," she told me. "The dynamics change when one of them is suddenly free."

The poet was much older, with a wife who had followed him from upheaval to upheaval—the kind of wife about whom you say "long-suffering," and leave it at that. There aren't really all that many types of people in this world. Live long enough and you meet them all, though it never surprises me how desperately people cling to their notion of uniqueness. "I didn't expect him to leave her, of course," Gertrudis said. "And I would have been quite mortified if he had." Gertrudis, of course, represented her own type.

At our next meeting, I gave her the documents I had drawn up. She told me there was no need for drama—she would serve them herself, at their home. She was about to leave when she sat down again and looked at me for a moment.

"You didn't ask me what I did after I found the tickets," she said.

I had assumed she had confronted her husband with them and told her so. She shook her head and smiled a little. "He still doesn't know that I have them," she said. "I imagine he's gone mad looking for them."

That night, after hiding the tickets in their copy of *The Problems of Philosophy*, Gertrudis had gone back to bed.

"I fell asleep almost immediately," she said. "And slept the night through."

She woke refreshed to find that her husband had already left for the day. She went to her office—she worked mostly at home—did some interviews, and then went shopping. At Epicure, she bought the makings of an elaborate meal: fresh scallops, a rack of lamb, rice for a risotto, and a chocolate tart. She spent the rest of the afternoon cooking, and when her husband returned home, she greeted him with a hot and delicious meal.

Hearing all this, I was becoming a bit nervous. It seemed to me that at best, Gertrudis had entered a dissociative state; at worst, she had planned to poison her husband. I interrupted her.

"I don't need to know all the details," I said.

Gertrudis looked at me, stunned, and I detected something behind her eyes. Hurt?

"What do you mean?" she said.

"I mean if there was any ... anything you did which you would have cause to regret ..."

She looked dumbfounded for a moment and then burst out laughing. "You think I put cyanide in the risotto?"

I smiled and shrugged. "Most women probably would have," I said.

"But I know nothing about poisonous chemicals," she said. "Words, on the other hand ..."

Mathieu was of course surprised to see the elaborate dinner. Perhaps he sensed that something was amiss, but like most of us, he probably fought off the feeling of unease. "What's this?" he asked.

"I've been neglecting you," Gertrudis responded. "We've both been working so hard and I can see how stressed you've been with all these recent trips and having to be away at Christmas. . . . I realize that I've been taking you for granted and I just want to say I'm sorry."

Her husband looked away. "Look," he said. "Don't be silly."

"No, really," she said. "We've been drifting apart and it's really my fault. I know I've been blaming you, but you've been wonderful, beyond fault really. It's me who has been distant and disengaged. I want to change that."

Mathieu became agitated. He alternated between anger and contrition. "Really, Gertrudis, now this is all nonsense." And the next moment, "Look, my love, I've been away too much." And again, the looking away, the flush of guilt on his neck.

Gertrudis had poured champagne. They ate. She continued her acts of contrition. She served the dessert. When she went to bed, he didn't follow; he said he had work to catch up with.

"It's no problem," she said.

He had another trip scheduled for the following week, which he canceled. Gertrudis continued her torture: cooking for him every night, flagellating herself for her failings, watching the guilt work on him like an acid.

"A change came over him," she said. "He began to linger in bed in the mornings. He told me he loved me. One night, he said simply, 'Gertrudis, I'm sorry for everything.'"

A month later, he told her he needed to fly to London for a meeting. He would be gone just three days. She offered to drive him to the airport, but as usual there was no need; the firm always sent a car.

The day of the flight, Gertrudis prepared him breakfast. She went down to the lobby with him to see him to his car. Then, instead of going back upstairs, she got into her own car and drove to the airport.

"They still had to pick up someone else, supposedly his boss," she said. "So I knew I would get there before them. I sat down with a cup of coffee at Versailles. I waited so long that I thought they might have changed gates. But then, I saw him coming through the door. Behind him was another person: his boss, just as he had said."

Gertrudis had waited to see if a third person joined them, but Mathieu didn't look around as if he were expecting anyone else. Both of them went straight to the kiosks to check in and then took their places in the security line. Gertrudis pivoted away on her bar stool, but it was unnecessary. Mathieu didn't once glance in her direction. The security line was long, and now and then Gertrudis could turn and watch her husband when his back was to her. So she saw when he took out his phone to make a call.

"A second later, my own phone rang," she said. "I almost picked it up, too, but then realized it would be a mistake."

After a while, he hung up and put the phone back in his pocket. A few moments later, the two men passed through security.

Gertrudis said she sat there for a long time, watching the travelers come and go, some happy, some sad, most of them displaying a numbed indifference.

Mathieu tried to reach her two more times before he boarded, but Gertrudis didn't pick up the phone. She waited until she saw that his plane had departed. And then, in the middle of the airport, she bowed her head.

It was her tears she was most ashamed of. She made me promise to never tell anyone that she had wept.

Voló Como Matías Pérez
by Rosaura del Bosque

Life is a dream from which death awakens
A journey taken on wingless flight
The land below a fleeting sight
Of love and pain so soon forsaken

For gull and sparrow he was mistaken
As he lifted silently to the sky
But Matías knew he would not fly
To any home on this old earth

His journey's only saving worth
Was escaping Newton's lie.

Traveling Fools
BY ZANEM NEENDA

All the men on my father's side of the family have been mad in one way or another.

There was my great-uncle Panchito, who joined the Communist Party in 1934, when it was a nothing party of dreamers, only to quit in 1965, when the party officially denied him permission to fly to the moon. He could have turned all those years of underground meetings and patriotic songs into something; he could have cashed in and finally helped his family. Instead, he spent the last years of his life writing angry letters to the Ministry of Travel and Culture, arguing that if the Russians could send a flea-bitten dog to space, certainly the Cubans ought to be able to send a loyal party monkey to the moon. His later letters were scrupulously ignored. And he ended up dying in a rented room in his niece's apartment, fighting her until the last for the right to his homemade rum. In the end, the party would not even allow him to be buried in the patriots' cemetery.

There was a cousin named Severino who hanged himself from a banyan one spring morning after a passing traveler told him there was buried treasure on the other side of the mountain. Severino, who had never even traveled beyond the swamp. As a boy he had been happy to sit out by a stream for hours and launch paper boats, waiting until each one disappeared downstream before sending out the next. The passing traveler was never seen or spoken of again until many years later, when miners discovered a silver vein hard against the mountain. The townspeople, in an act of remembering common in those times, named the mine after Severino.

And, most recently, there was my grandfather Solomon, who, as an exile in Miami, one cool winter morning began digging a tunnel beneath the azaleas with the intention of surfacing someday in Havana.

The first two stories have been passed down through the family and I can't vouch for their truth. The last one I saw with my own eyes, and I can tell you that nothing can match the image of a shirtless old man with a dream. He had it all planned out, my grandfather did, for he was a man who took great pride in logic and the scientific method. Before he even began to dig, he filled a great many notebooks with figures that explained precisely how many shovels of dirt it would take, how wide the hole should be, and how many years would have to pass before he finally broke through the sand on the other side.

I was only eight years old then, but sometimes after school I helped him dig. My grandfather had barely made it under the property line when his project ended abruptly. It seems the neighbors had called the police to say the old man next door was digging what appeared to be a mass grave. It took some days to sort out the complications that followed. But my grandfather never recovered from his disappointment. He sank into a deep sadness that didn't lift even after my father, also prone to making mathematical calculations, pointed out a mistake in his figures and said that it actually would have taken 16,742 years to dig to Havana.

But perhaps the most tragically brilliant of this mad lineage was Matías Padrón, a third great-cousin of my father's through marriage by way of his mother. The family connection is tenuous, I know. But I feel a certain pride in claiming Matías, for his story has passed into the island lore of Cuba; his story is our story.

Matías, so it is told, was not a very big man. This is also true of most of the men on my father's side of the family. But unlike most of the men, who tend to make up in width for what they lack in height, Matías was slightly built all around. He was, it is well known, even smaller and thinner than his wife, who scandalously abused her advantage to keep Matías timid and soft-spoken at home. Matías didn't seem to mind this and often played along good-naturedly, now and then repeating a favorite phrase he had heard about the greatness of a man being measured not from the ground to his head, but from the distance of his head to God. The literal-minded took this to be an even greater disadvantage. But Matías knew what he was talking about.

Since he had turned eighteen, Matías had been running the post office in Santiago de Cuba. By the time he was forty years old, he had browsed through twenty-two Christmas catalogs from El Encanto, leafed through dozens of *Bohemia*s, and read several hundred letters of love, the great majority of which were not between husbands and wives. But the task that took up most of his time—and the one that, by all accounts, he adored above all the others—was predicting the weather. In those years, the postmaster also ran the local telegraph service. This meant that the postmaster, in addition to being the telegrapher, was also a sort of informal meteorologist, as the telegraph, for the first time in the Caribbean, was being used to give advance warnings of storms developing offshore. It was a duty that all the previous postmasters had taken very seriously. But none had thrown themselves into it with anything approaching the passion that Matías brought.

Matías and his wife lived above the post office in a house that, according to tradition, was paid and kept up by the municipality for the use of the postmaster and his family. It was a large house, two stories, with a wide balcony that wrapped around all four sides. But as Matías and his wife had never had children, vast areas of the house remained dark and unused. It was in one such sealed room that Matías established a small office. When he wasn't below in the post office reading other people's mail or receiving telegraphs about the latest events around the world, Matías was in his little office, trying to predict the weather. He had all manner of instruments—barometers, thermometers. Probably, these weren't too different from the types of things amateurs keep the world over. But Matías's secrecy about his room, even with his wife, soon led to talk in the town that Matías was an alchemist dealing in nefarious activities. It was the first chatter about Matías's supposed eccentricity. And although it prefigured the extraordinary act he was about to embark on, this doesn't mean that it was necessarily a fair assessment. At the moment,

I believe that Matías had truly developed a scientific interest in the weather. After all, not too many years had passed since a hurricane had devastated Varadero, cutting the narrow peninsula in half until both oceans met over the sand. Matías, I think, was trying to save Santiago from the next cataclysm.

He ordered all manner of new equipment from New York and tore at the packages when they arrived weeks later. Soon he built an observation deck on the roof, and in clear weather began sending up weather balloons. At first, the balloons didn't carry anything—Matías merely used them to calculate wind speeds and air pressure. But as technology improved and radio transmitters began to gain wider currency, Matías arranged for bigger and bigger balloons that could carry more and more equipment. Soon he was launching balloons as big as oil drums carrying the thermometers, the barometers, and the humidity detectors, all wired to a radio that could send the information back to Matías in his little room.

Every Friday, he posted the results on the front door of the post office, as well as a brief assessment of what the coming week's weather was likely to be. He was right more often than he was wrong, and except for a few lapses when, for example, he announced that yesterday's "rain had been very heavy" (something the townspeople could know well enough without consulting any instruments other than their memories), the people grew to respect his forecasts.

Cuba had prospered in those years and along with it, Santiago, and along with Santiago, Matías. The memory of hunger was fading. Children grew fat. And Matías entered middle age in the prime of health. Even the hurricanes that had assaulted Cuba during the previous decade eased, and everyone everywhere seemed relaxed and content as if the more malevolent workings of the world had finally passed the Cubans by.

Matías continued to go into his office every afternoon, and every Friday he emerged with the forecast for the following week. And of course he also continued to send up his balloons, each more elaborate than the last. The weather was not always perfect, but it was predictable. Soon everyone knew the rains would come in August and the heaviest thunder would be reserved for the late afternoon, when the sun began to dip low in the sky. By October, the skies would clear and the blue days return. Winters, whether Matías said so or not, were generally dry and pleasant.

Some nights, couples out for a walk noticed a dark figure above the post office—Matías, with his hands on the railing looking up into the sky. But otherwise, few people paid much attention to Matías or his forecasts anymore. They met him once a week, sometimes touched their fingers lightly to his when he handed them their mail, and that was that. It seemed there was nothing left to fear.

~

There are eddies that develop in time, places where histories converge and individuals caught inside the current find themselves suddenly unable to act for themselves. Perhaps this is what happened to Matías. Maybe everything that followed was as inevitable as history. I have to say things like this because there is really no other explanation for what came to pass. Except for a family connection, there was nothing in Matías's character to suggest madness. The reports that emerged later pointed out that there was no history of despondency. And nothing in the days preceding the event gave anyone any reason to believe that Matías had suffered a sudden depression. The weather, moreover, had been pleasantly uneventful, with, as Matías himself had noted, an abundance of bright days somewhat unusual for springtime.

And yet, the truth is this: One morning Matías was handing a stack of letters to Consuelo Peréz, and the next he was floating high above Santiago, his office chair, with him in it, dangling beneath four giant weather balloons.

Santiago had been the first city in Cuba to be linked by telegraph to the rest of the Caribbean. Santiago had been the first city to pioneer the use of observation balloons during wartime. The telegraph had connected Cuba to the world, but in the end, the country learned it could not stand alone. Its prosperity and health were forever tethered to history and geography. Did Matías sense this? In those last years he had developed a habit of linking ideas one to the next until he'd convinced himself that there was an inherent logic running through the universe, governing even the impossible. When his own mind finally became untethered, where did it fly?

His wife was the first to notice Matías had gone. She ran up to the observation deck, and when she saw him just clearing the tops of the palms she began to shout at him, "You insolent madman! You flying fool!" Her shouting brought out a handful of people whose shouting brought out still more people. And soon the whole town was pointing at the sky where Matías floated, sometimes rising suddenly and sometimes hanging in the air, swaying from side to side just over the tree line, every second becoming a bit smaller in the distance. A few of the men started off after him and when they were directly under his path, began shouting instructions at him, in the venerable Cuban tradition: "Cut one of the balloons! Jump now, the fronds will break your fall! When you make it over the swamp, let the helium out very slowly!" They continued to run and shout even after it became clear that Matías was not coming back. One of the men said that just when he was becoming so small that one could hardly make out his person, Matías glanced down at the others and there was a wide, white smile on his face. He was like a saint or a martyr, the man said. And for days, the man could talk of nothing else but Matías's calm happy gaze as he floated away from Santiago forever.

Matías seemed to know right where he was going. All those years of tracing wind patterns had given him a pilot's confidence. It was April, when the winds blow east to west. Before an hour had passed, he was a tiny speck out over the sea and then he was impossible to make out in the haze. After a while most of the people stopped searching the sky for Matías and began walking back to their homes. A few gathered in silence outside the post office. Matilde locked herself in the house and didn't emerge until the governor arrived two weeks later to take a report. Some days later, the police came for Matías's papers. They carted off hundreds and hundreds of notebooks filled with indecipherable drawings and algebraic calculations. Among the more curious of his possessions were a stuffed owl and a rare Cuban tern preserved in a bottle of formaldehyde.

Today, people in Cuba still say of an elusive fellow, "He vanished like Matías Padrón."

~

I think of Matías now and then. I am also a traveler. And nowadays after I have taken off my shoes and put them back on, after I have retrieved my naked laptop from the conveyor and had my purse rifled through, after I have emerged safely on the other side of the security cabal, I like to take a seat up close to the windows and watch the planes come and go. How generous of airport architects to design such large windows. And how good of the staff to keep them so clean and shiny. Coming upon these portals is like stumbling on a new and intricate explanation of the possible.

I sit in one of the soft functional chairs and watch the planes land and watch them lift off from the earth. And each time it seems like a miracle. There are so many planes flying in so many different directions that it is difficult to follow a single one. Too often, the flight path takes them beyond my line of vision. But now and then a plane will take off just so and fly straight out in view of all the airport, fly off to that point that everyone calls infinity but is really just the limit of our perception.

I'll follow the plane until it is nothing and know that soon I will be on one just like it. And I wonder: Do we still know what it's like to dream about the other side of the mountain? At what point does one cross the crest of forgetting? And this is when I think of Matías, who breached the space of the known for nothing more than a glimpse of the white-blind city on the other side.

The Shunting Trains Trace Iron Labyrinths
BY ANA MENÉNDEZ

I boarded the train and took the last empty seat, by the window. Outside it was snowing. There was an announcement in three languages, none of which I understood. The woman next to me was eating a bowl of black beans. Seeing my confusion she turned to me and said, "This train goes to the coast." I thanked her. More people came on board. There was shouting, and much shoving. Men were forced to stand in the aisles. After a while, the car began to move. On the platform, those left behind shook their fists. Two men in long coats ran along the edge waving at the conductor and pointing to the car where I sat. They wore identical black hats and looked like brothers, except that one was bearded and the other hairless. I understood then that they would follow me wherever I went, would follow me unto death.

Outside, dawn had returned, but brought with it little light. The sky was low and gray, though still studded with faint candlelight. The train picked up speed. Dirty snow was piled along both sides of the tracks. We were moving through a bare landscape empty of trees and homes. The only structures were enormous steel pylons arranged in rows, going into the smoky distance. The woman pointed to the place where the parallel rows met and said, "That's where we're going." Her name was

Gertrude. I repeated the name to her. But she said she had never seen me before, that I must have her confused with someone else. She had come from a city farther north and had been traveling for several days, trying to reach the coast like the others. "Everyone here is an emigrant," she explained. "We're all going to the same place." The train rocked and I slept. After an indefinite time, I was woken by another announcement, repeated in the three strange languages. I waited for Gertrude to translate it, but she didn't. I asked her how they passed the time on the train. "Only waiting," she said. "And sometimes they play a movie." She pointed to the tattered screens hanging at the front of the car. "But it's always the same one." Three times a day, by however a day was measured, the dining car opened, Gertrude told me. But they always served the same thing.

After a time, I asked Gertrude the question I feared most: "When will we be arriving?" Gertrude shrugged. "It's up to the conductor." "Who is the conductor?" "No one knows," she replied. Before she fell asleep she said, "Some of us have been traveling for years and we still don't know."

I, too, had been traveling for years. In the summer of my thirty-seventh year, I set out from home without a destination or goal. I was weary of inventions and the lies needed to sustain them. The things that passed for reality no longer animated me: the simulated conversations, the blue light at twilight, landscapes brushed with premonition. These all stopped meaning anything; and the world that I had made for myself, that had once, at its creation, filled me with hope, now collapsed into hollow space.

I woke one morning to realize that all about me was void, that it was I who had invented sound, light, color, love, shame. I had made the red and the black. The good and bad. The telling abstraction as well as the showing detail, which was really (I now saw) the cleverest and most insidious lie ever told. Worse than this, I understood now, with perfect horror, that I had also invented other people. Everyone I loved and hated, every pompous rich man I ever knew, every poor laborer was mine and was me. The leper for whom I refused to lower the window. The boy who dreamed of flight. The glamorous stranger I met in Istanbul. The cook with a failed dream was really me on the cusp of adulthood, full of fire and feeling so as not to know that I was unloved and alone. The world was an illusion, sustained by my need to make it whole. This knowledge came upon me slowly, over many weeks, even years, until I understood its source: He and I were in a courtyard in a grand building by the river. Piano music came through an open window. We slipped through the gated entry and walked in slow circles until we had found the exact window, four floors up. A recording, he whispered. But different from any he had heard. Chopin, the second concerto, composed when the pianist was just twenty years old. Rubinstein? But no, there was a lightness to it, an unusual buoyancy. It was a summer evening, all rich light and fragrant wind. The treetops were themselves in mad and hopeless love and the stars strained at their portholes to look down on us. And then the pianist stumbled, hit a wrong note, stopped. The silence lasted a full measure. The man turned his face down and shook his head. Only someone practicing, he said. But I stood fast, transformed. The flaw. The imperfection. That stumble and the silence that came after were the only true things. I have been a traveler ever since.

The train pulled us along, tireless. We crossed one sea and then another. The landscape changed from jungle to desert and back again. Details are stupid and unreal. Don't get sucked in by my lies. There was only sand and sand and sand. It blew in the afternoons, toward evening, with the most mournful howling you'll ever hear. It shook the cars of the train, a wind strong enough to unhorn goats.

On the third day, Gertrude brought me black beans from the dining car. She told me that she had once lived by the sea. As a young woman, she had taken many lovers, and they all died. She had a child with a poet, who left her before the child was born. The child also died. She married another poet, and he died. She married again and divorced for no reason. "Look," she said. "The movie's begun."

On the tattered screen appeared the familiar scene: A border zone. A man jumping over barbed wire. A family on a picnic learns of a teenager shot while trying to escape. A balloon will be built. The images had worn holes in the canvas.

"I've seen this," I said.

"Of course," said Gertrude. "All the stories are the same: We're always leaving."

We watched the movie until the last credits because there was nothing else to do. I ate my beans and slept. After a time, the weather grew warm. I opened the window above me. We had left the desert and entered a new land. I told Gertrude that I could smell the sea, and she laughed. Later, a man came through the aisles, pushing and shoving those who were standing. At the entrance to the car, he stopped and threw a handful of black beans at us.

"With these beans I redeem myself and mine," he said.

"The cook," said Gertrude. "He does this once a year, though no one understands why."

"How long have we been traveling?" I asked Gertrude.

"Impossible to say," she said.

I stood and told her I was going to speak to the conductor. She laughed again, but didn't stop me. I had to push my way through the aisle to the front of the car. I passed into another car identical to mine. Again, I pushed my way up the aisle. Men and women filled every seat. Near the front, a little boy sat crying next to his mother, who slept beside him, unmoved. I passed into the next car, this one identical to the one before. Again, I had to push my way through the people in the aisle.

"Where is the conductor?" I asked. But no one seemed to understand me.

The next car was full of young men, each sitting by himself, staring ahead or out the window. Not a word was spoken among them, each having cast his lot with this world's most solitary spirits. I left the car quickly and passed into another car, again identical to the ones I had left behind.

"How many cars are in this train?" I asked, but no one replied.

In the next car, four women sat close together, talking quietly. The oldest among them lifted her head and saw me. Suddenly she stood and began to shout at me, pointing with a book she held in her hand. The others stood as well. Their tone was aggrieved, accusatory, but I could not understand the words.

"It's not me," I said. "I'm not the conductor."

Some of the men in the car stood and began to walk toward me. The women continued to shout, pointing fingers and appealing to the others for some sort of justice. I pushed through the aisle, leaving the crowd behind, and came to another car. This one was full of white horses. They stood alone, calmly. It was the quietest of cars. As I passed, they stepped aside to give me room. I had grown tired and wanted to sleep there among those gentle horses, but I knew I must push on to the front, where the conductor waited with the secret of our destination.

I slid open the door to the next car and was overcome by the smell of garlic and onions. A great vat of black beans bubbled in the middle of the car, stirred by the little cook, who mumbled to himself in Latin. All around the pot, the others stood, bowls in hand: men, women, children. Some wore smart city clothing, but most were in the rough trousers and shirts of the countryside. They seemed to be shouting, but I could not hear them over the music that blared from unseen speakers: the opening notes of the same danzón played over and over again. I struggled to push through them and after many hours at last succeeded.

In the next car I was sure to find the conductor. But it was another car like the others: the same people in the seats, the same men crowding the aisle, and in the fourth row from the front, Gertrude sitting next to an empty space, my own.

"Did you find the conductor?" she asked me with a smile.

I sat, exhausted. Later that evening there was another announcement in three languages. Gertrude said simply, "We are headed for the coast."

Through days and nights we moved, not stopping for snow or heat. Our route seemed to cut through the center of this country, crisscrossing abandoned cities, ancient forests, jungles of fern and roses. Mine seems to have been the last station. One morning we passed an army truck full of sleeping soldiers, but otherwise the landscape was empty of living things. Just miles and miles of land and sky. Along the side of the track grew brown bushes studded with colored bits of paper and plastic. The train rocked from side to side like a fugitive raft on the deep sea. When it was hot, the people slept. In the cold, they moved close to each other, sharing their soup with the children. Now and then a distant whistle blew. Sometimes smoke from the engine was sucked back in through the windows, unraveling the thousand and one stories on that train.

All who create will find one day the need to destroy. See the shining husband with the beautiful wife. He will drink. Or he will pretend to take business trips. Like all of us, he began his life with hope. And then in the middle of it, he begins to take it all down, piece by piece. The flawless beauty of it is too much to bear. We abandon our cities and our ambitions. At the first sign of boredom we take to the air. Beware the pursuit of perfection that casts its shadow-self over everything it denies. Better to pass through this life in the night, leaving no fingerprints, like a thief who does it for joy.

One day, toward evening, I woke to the sound of tinkling bells. Shards of light cut through the dusty air of our car. We had entered some kind of endless rail yard. Twenty paces from our train, a parallel train raced, bound for the same destination. And behind that, another train farther in the distance, and behind that one . . . We stood and opened the windows and the passengers in the other trains did the same. We waved and they returned the wave. We shouted into the absolute silence of that watery landscape and heard only our own voices repeated. We were still miles from the coast, and alone. The others were an illusion. We were only passing through a wilderness of mirrors, startling ourselves on the way back to the beginning.

Contributors' Notes

Johnny Aldo was the pen name of a popular writer of horoscopes —or, as he preferred to call them, "zodiacs." He suffered from a rare neurological condition—lipogrammaticus extremis—that prevents its victims from using certain letters of the alphabet. In Johnny's case, this was the letter "e." Early in his life, he was drawn to spirituality after noticing that none of the world's major religions contained the dreaded letter. He forms part of a notable clan of eccentrics documented in the 1984 book *The Family of Constraints.*

Laika Almeida was born in Havana in 1992. "The Boy Who Fell from Heaven" is his first published story.

Marta Yara Baldwin was born in Oriente and as a young girl wanted to be a train conductor. She is today an art history professor who divides her time between Boston and Pittsburgh.

Alex Carpenter is the Swiss-born third cousin twice removed of the renowned Cuban writer with whom he shares a resemblance in both name and writing style. Having failed to achieve the fame of his celebrated relative, Alex emigrated to Miami, where he still lives, the owner of a pharmacy in Little Havana.

C. Casey—the granddaughter of one of the most important astrophysicists of the Cold War generation—received her PhD in art history from Emory University. While at Emory, she met Italo Calvino, the Italian writer born in Havana, who persuaded her that you didn't need to be Cuban to write about Cubans or vice versa.

Celestino d'Alba began writing at the age of two. By the time he was five, he had covered the leaves of all the banana trees in his grandfather's plantation with verse. For this and other crimes, he was heavily persecuted and harassed until forced to flee to New York City, where he died.

Teresa de la Landre, a poet and revolutionary, is unfortunately best remembered as a painter who faked a relationship with Ernesto "Che" Guevara. She died in Havana during the "Special Period" after falling from the roof of her building in the Vedado. Though the death was officially ruled a suicide, her daughter maintained until the end that Teresa had planned to fly to Miami and simply forgot her wings.

Rosaura del Bosque, an aunt of Johnny Aldo's, was one of the materfamilias of *The Family of Constraints*. Though trained as a medical doctor, she preferred to spend her time writing historical poetry and pursuing eccentric medical theories that embarrassed her family, including one positing that cancer cells actually were an alien invasionary force from the Andromeda galaxy. She died in 2012 of a rare carcinoma of the Bellini ducts.

Ernesto del Camino was born in Miami, the son of Cuban ex-iles. In college, he worked briefly as a freelance copy editor at the local newspaper, and he would forever be marked by this early choice. He went on to study for a PhD in comparative literature: his thesis involved going through the novels of Er-nest Hemingway and correcting the awkward English that was supposed to imitate Spanish, but that to his mind just reeked of lazy translation. He thought it laughable that characters who very obviously speak in Spanish should appear to be speaking English. But he reserved his wrath for the trend—especially in vogue in the 1990s—of interspersing bits of Spanish into novels written in English. Ernesto's ideas were, of course, very provoca-tive, and got him invited to many literature conferences, where he inevitably got into scuffles.

Vietor Fúka, a meteorologist and philologist, was born in Malacky, Czechoslovakia, in 1937. A champion sailor and kite-surfer, Fúka had been obsessed with the wind and the sea since childhood. In addition to *Glossary of Caribbean Winds*, excerpted here, he is also the author of the 1,000-page *Dictionary of Tides*, a combination of poetry and reference, which has never been equaled.

Carla Gades, a cookbook author, psychiatrist, and poet of the twentieth century, was heavily influenced by the Italian avant-garde. She spent the last twenty years of her life working on her most ambitious project, *How to Cook a Fractal*, which, had she finished it, would have revolutionized the cookbook industry. The book opens with a simple recipe for ganache and then grows exponentially, following the principles laid down by the Fibonacci series. She is said to have come upon the idea for the book after buying a head of Romanesco broccoli at a market in Rome. *How to Cook a Fractal* remained unfinished—at 3,307 pages—at the time of her death. Most of her other works have since been forgotten, or co-opted by later, minor writers.

Gertrudis Gómez—who is no relation to the Cuban poet of the same name—is a former journalist and author.

Silas Haslam is the author of *A General History of Labyrinths*, a monumental work that continues to be cited to this day (see A. Hagberg and E. Meron, "Order Parameter Equations for Front Transitions: Nonuniformly Curved Fronts," *Physica D*, November 15, 1998). He seems to have published very few short stories in his lifetime; of these, "The Poet in His Labyrinth" is believed to be the only one extant.

Joseph Martin, a promising poet in his twenties, turned to translation in his thirties, declaring that all the good poems had already been written.

Ana Menéndez is the pseudonym of an imaginary writer and translator, invented, if not to lend coherence to this collection, at least to offer it the pretense of contemporary relevance.

Zanem Neenda was born in Miami in 1974, the great-grand-daughter (on her mother's side) of Lebanese refugees who had fled the breakup of the Ottoman Empire via Ireland on *The March Warbler*. On her father's side she is distantly related to Johnny Aldo.

Victoria O'Campo, the Argentine editor, was instrumental in reintroducing the works of forgotten sixteenth-century Irish poets to the Spanish-speaking world. After *A Brief History of the Cuban Poets* was published, she was attacked in the Cuban press for "knowing nothing about nothing." Her anthology was declared "unserious," "superficial," and "just plain wrong," and she was forced to flee to Iceland, where she dedicated the rest of her life to the study of reindeer.

Nitza Pol-Villa was not a Communist.

Herberto Quain, an Irish author, was born in Roscommon. He settled in Havana as a young man and never left. His most well-known work, *The God of the Labyrinth*, is no longer in print.

Ovid Rodrigues, a poet and historian specializing in vanished civilizations of the Sierra Maestra, divides his time between New Aquilo and Havana, where much of his research takes him to the National Library. It is here that he first became acquainted with Herberto Quain, who found him a publisher for his first works. Contrary to popular belief, Ovid was not named after the Roman poet. His father was a mathematician who delighted in word games. Thus, the name he gave his firstborn son is an anagram of the English word "void."

Jane Smith is the heteronym of a Cuban attorney who has lived and worked in Miami for many years. A champion skydiver, she briefly held the world record for longest free fall.

Acknowledgments

Boundless thanks to my editor, Elisabeth Schmitz, who always understands what I'm trying to say better than I do. It's good to be back. And to my agent, Joy Harris, whose extraordinary dedication to my work is always far out of proportion to her remuneration. At the Joy Harris Literary Agency, special thanks to Adam Reed and Sarah Twombly, whose intelligent suggestions improve anything I write.

To Alan Cheuse, who continues to be mentor, friend, and benevolent godfather, my everlasting gratitude. Ileana Oroza remains a world-class friend and editor—many thanks for her face-saving edits to "Un Cuento Extraño." Any errors that remain are my own or, better still, deliberate.

The seeds of this book were planted in Cairo, and I'm grateful for the support of the Binational Fulbright Commission in Egypt and especially to the incomparable Bruce Lohof and his wife, Annemarie, who offered friendship, hospitality, and a space for wonder and exploration.

I'm grateful, as ever, for the support of my family: my parents, Maria and Saul; my sister, Rose; her husband, Gio; and their three beautiful monkeys: Elle, Rocco, and Scarlett.

The courage, foolhardiness, and resilience of Cuba's poets down the ages is a constant source of inspiration. This book is dedicated to all of them, especially to the first Cuban poet in my life: my uncle, Dionisio Martinez. With hopes that he will forgive me for calling him a Cuban poet.

I am forever in debt to Peter, for his love, his support, and his superhuman ability to listen to the same stories over and over again. Under your care I have laughed and lived as never before. Thank you for giving me wings.